They brought in Joiry's tall commander, struggling between the men-at-arms, who tightly gripped the ropes which bound their captive's mailed arms. They picked their way between mounds of dead as they crossed the great hall towards the dais where the conquerors sat, and twice they slipped a little in the blood that spattered the flags. When they came to a halt before the mailed figure on the dais, Joiry's commander was breathing hard, and the voice that echoed hollowly under the helmet's confines was hoarse with fury and despair.

Guillaume the conqueror leaned on his mighty sword . . . "Unshell me this lobster," said Guillaume in his deep, lazy voice. "We'll see what sort of face the fellow has who gave us such a battle. Off with his helmet, you."

The helmet rolled on the flagstones. Guillaume's white teeth clicked on a startled oath. He stared. Joiry's lady glared back at him from between her captors, wild red hair tousled, wild lion-yellow eyes ablaze.

"God curse you," snarled the lady of Joiry between clenched teeth. "God blast your black heart."

Ace Books by C. L. Moore

JIREL OF JOIRY
NORTHWEST SMITH

with Henry Kuttner
EARTH'S LAST CITADEL

JIREL OF JOIRY

C. L. MOORE

Published in a limited hardcover edition as <u>Black God's Shadow</u>

ACE BOOKS, NEW YORK

ACKNOWLEDGMENTS

Black God's Kiss, copyright 1934, 1961 by Weird Tales, Inc.
Black God's Shadow, copyright 1934, 1961 by Weird Tales, Inc.
The Dark Land, copyright 1936, 1963 by Weird Tales, Inc.
Hellsgarde, copyright 1939, 1966 by Weird Tales, Inc.
Jirel Meets Magic, copyright 1935, 1962 by Weird Tales, Inc.

JIREL OF JOIRY

An Ace Book / published by arrangement with the author

ISBN: 0-441-38570-2

ACE®
Ace Books are published by The Berkley Publishing Group,
200 Madison Avenue, New York, New York 10016.
ACE and the "A" design
are trademarks belonging to Charter Communications, Inc.

PRINTED IN THE UNITED STATES OF AMERICA

Contents

JIREL OF JOIRY

Black God's Kiss

I

They brought in Joiry's tall commander, struggling between two men-at-arms who tightly gripped the ropes which bound their captive's mailed arms. They picked their way between mounds of dead as they crossed the great hall toward the dais where the conqueror sat, and twice they slipped a little in the blood that spattered the flags. When they came to a halt before the mailed figure on the dais, Joiry's commander was breathing hard, and the voice that echoed hollowly under the helmet's confines was hoarse with fury and despair.

Guillaume the conqueror leaned on his mighty sword, hands crossed on its hilt, grinning down from his height upon the furious captive before him. He was a big man, Guillaume, and he looked bigger still in his spattered armor. There was blood on his hard, scarred face, and he was grinning a white grin that split his short, curly beard glitteringly. Very splendid and very dangerous he looked, leaning on his great sword and smiling down upon fallen Joiry's lord, struggling between the stolid men-at-arms.

"Unshell me this lobster," said Guillaume in his deep, lazy voice. "We'll see what sort of face the fellow has who gave us such a battle. Off with his helmet, you."

But a third man had to come up and slash the straps which held the iron helmet on, for the struggles of Joiry's commander were too fierce, even with bound arms, for either of the guards to release their hold. There was a moment of sharp struggle; then the straps parted and the helmet rolled loudly across the flagstones.

Guillaume's white teeth clicked on a startled oath. He stared. Joiry's lady glared back at him from between her captors, wild red hair tousled, wild lion-yellow eyes ablaze.

"God curse you!" snarled the lady of Joiry between clenched teeth. "God blast your black heart!"

Guillaume scarcely heard her. He was still staring, as most men stared when they first set eyes upon Jirel of Joiry. She was tall as most men, and as savage as the wildest of them, and the fall of Joiry was bitter enough to break her heart as she stood snarling curses up at her tall conqueror. The face above her mail might not have been fair in a woman's head-dress, but in the steel setting of her armor it had a biting, sword-edge beauty as keen as the flash of blades. The red hair was short upon her high, defiant head, and the yellow blaze of her eyes held fury as a crucible holds fire.

Guillaume's stare melted into a slow smile. A little

light kindled behind his eyes as he swept the long, strong lines of her with a practised gaze. The smile broadened, and suddenly he burst into full-throated laughter, a deep bull bellow of amusement and delight.

"By the Nails!" he roared. "Here's welcome for the warrior! And what forfeit d'ye offer, pretty one, for your life?"

She blazed a curse at him.

"So? Naughty words for a mouth so fair, my lady. Well, we'll not deny you put up a gallant battle. No man could have done better, and many have done worse. But against Guillaume—" He inflated his splendid chest and grinned down at her from the depths of his jutting beard. "Come to me, pretty one," he commanded. "I'll wager your mouth is sweeter than your words."

Jirel drove a spurred heel into the shin of one guard and twisted from his grip as he howled, bringing up an iron knee into the abdomen of the other. She had writhed from their grip and made three long strides toward the door before Guillaume caught her. She felt his arms closing about her from behind, and lashed out with both spiked heels in a futile assault upon his leg armor, twisting like a maniac, fighting with her knees and spurs, straining hopelessly at the ropes which bound her arms. Guillaume laughed and whirled her round, grinning down into the blaze of her yellow eyes. Then deliberately he set a fist under her chin and tilted her mouth up to his. There was a cessation of her hoarse curses.

"By Heaven, that's like kissing a sword-blade," said Guillaume, lifting his lips at last.

Jirel choked something that was mercifully muffled

as she darted her head sidewise, like a serpent striking, and sank her teeth into his neck. She missed the jugular by a fraction of an inch.

Guillaume said nothing, then. He sought her head with a steady hand, found it despite her wild writhing, sank iron fingers deep into the hinges of her jaw, forcing her teeth relentlessly apart. When he had her free he glared down into the yellow hell of her eyes for an instant. The blaze of them was hot enough to scorch his scarred face. He grinned and lifted his ungauntleted hand, and with one heavy blow in the face he knocked her half-way across the room. She lay still upon the flags.

II

Jirel opened her yellow eyes upon darkness. She lay quiet for a while, collecting her scattered thoughts. By degrees it came back to her, and she muffled upon her arm a sound that was half curse and half sob. Joiry had fallen. For a time she lay rigid in the dark, forcing herself to the realization.

The sound of feet shifting on stone near by brought her out of that particular misery. She sat up cautiously, feeling about her to determine in what part of Joiry its liege lady was imprisoned. She knew that the sound she had heard must be a sentry, and by the dank smell of the darkness that she was underground. In one of the little dungeon cells, of course. With careful quietness she got to her feet, muttering a curse as her head reeled for an instant and then began to throb. In the utter dark she felt around the cell. Presently she came to a little wooden stool in a corner, and was satisfied. She gripped one leg of it with firm fingers and made her soundless way around the wall until she had located the door.

The sentry remembered, afterward, that he had heard the wildest shriek for help which had ever rung in his ears, and he remembered unbolting the door. Afterward, until they found him lying inside the locked cell with a cracked skull, he remembered nothing.

Jirel crept up the dark stairs of the north turret, murder in her heart. Many little hatreds she had known in her life, but no such blaze as this. Before her eyes in the night she could see Guillaume's scornful, scarred face laughing, the little jutting beard split with the whiteness of his mirth. Upon her mouth she felt the remembered weight of his, about her the strength of his arms. And such a blast of hot fury came over her that she reeled a little and clutched at the wall for support. She went on in a haze of red anger, and something like madness burning in her brain as a resolve slowly took shape out of the chaos of her hate. When that thought came to her she paused again, mid-step upon the stairs, and was conscious of a little coldness blowing over her. Then it was gone, and she shivered a little, shook her shoulders and grinned wolfishly, and went on.

By the stars she could see through the arrow-slits in the wall it must be near to midnight. She went softly on the stairs, and she encountered no one. Her little tower room at the top was empty. Even the straw pallet where the serving-wench slept had not been used that night. Jirel got herself out of her armor alone, somehow, after much striving and twisting. Her doeskin shirt was stiff with sweat and stained blood. She tossed it disdainfully into a corner. The fury in her eyes had cooled now to a contained and secret flame. She smiled to herself as she slipped a fresh shirt of doeskin over her tousled red head and donned a brief tunic of link-mail. On her legs she buckled the greaves of some forgotten legionary, relic of the not long past days when Rome still ruled the world. She thrust a dagger through her belt and took her own long two-handed sword bare-bladed in her grip. Then she went down the stairs again.

She knew there must have been revelry and feasting in the great hall that night, and by the silence hanging so heavily now she was sure that most of her enemies lay still in drunken slumber, and she experienced a swift regret for the gallons of her good French wine so wasted. And the thought flashed through her head that a determined woman with a sharp sword might work some little damage among the drunken sleepers before she was overpowered. But she put that idea by, for Guillaume would have posted sentries to spare, and she must not give up her secret freedom so fruitlessly.

Down the dark stairs she went, and crossed one corner of the vast central hall whose darkness she was sure hid wine-deadened sleepers, and so into the lesser dimness of the rough little chapel that Joiry boasted. She had been sure she would find Father Gervase there, and she was not mistaken. He rose from his knees before the altar, dark in his robe, the starlight through the narrow window shining upon his tonsure.

"My daughter!" he whispered. "My daughter! How have you escaped? Shall I find you a mount? If you can pass the sentries you should be in your cousin's castle by daybreak."

She hushed him with a lifted hand.

"No," she said. "It is not outside I go this night. I have a more perilous journey even than that to make. Shrive me, father."

He stared at her.

"What is it?"

She dropped to her knees before him and gripped the rough cloth of his habit with urgent fingers.

"Shrive me, I say! I go down into hell tonight to pray the devil for a weapon, and it may be I shall not return."

Gervase bent and gripped her shoulders with hands that shook.

"Look at me!" he demanded. "Do you know what you're saying? You go—"

"Down!" She said it firmly. "Only you and I know that passage, father—and not even we can be sure of what lies beyond. But to gain a weapon against that man I would venture into perils even worse than that."

"If I thought you meant it," he whispered, "I would waken Guillaume now and give you into his arms. It would be a kinder fate, my daughter."

"It's that I would walk through hell to escape," she whispered back fiercely. "Can't you see? Oh, God knows I'm not innocent of the ways of light loving— but to be any man's fancy, for a night or two, before he snaps my neck or sells me into slavery—and above all, if that man were Guillaume! Can't you understand?"

"That would be shame enough," nodded Gervase. "But think, Jirel! For that shame there is atonement and absolution, and for that death the gates of heaven open wide. But this other—Jirel, Jirel, never through all eternity may you come out, body or soul, if you venture—down!"

She shrugged.

"To wreak my vengeance upon Guillaume I would go if I knew I should burn in hell for ever."

"But Jirel, I do not think you understand. This is a worse fate than the deepest depths of hell-fire. This is—this is beyond all the bounds of the hells we know. And I think Satan's hottest flames were the breath of paradise, compared to what may befall there."

"I know. Do you think I'd venture down if I could not be sure? Where else would I find such a weapon as I need, save outside God's dominion?"

"Jirel, you shall not!"

"Gervase, I go! Will you shrive me?" The hot yellow eyes blazed into his, lambent in the starlight.

After a moment he dropped his head. "You are my lady. I will give you God's blessing, but it will not avail you—there."

III

She went down into the dungeons again. She went down a long way through utter dark, over stones that were oozy and odorous with moisture, through blackness that had never known the light of day. She might have been a little afraid at other times, but that steady flame of hatred burning behind her eyes was a torch to light the way, and she could not wipe from her memory the feel of Guillaume's arms about her, the scornful press of his lips on her mouth. She whimpered a little, low in her throat, and a hot gust of hate went over her.

In the solid blackness she came at length to a wall, and she set herself to pulling the loose stones from this with her free hand, for she would not lay down the sword. They had never been laid in mortar, and they came out easily. When the way was clear she stepped through and found her feet upon a downward-sloping ramp of smooth stone. She cleared the rubble away from the hole in the wall, and enlarged it enough for a quick passage; for when she came back this way—if she did—it might well be that she would come very fast.

At the bottom of the slope she dropped to her knees on the cold floor and felt about. Her fingers traced the outline of a circle, the veriest crack in the stone. She felt until she found the ring in its center. That ring was of the coldest metal she had ever known, and the smoothest. She could put no name to it. The daylight had never shone upon such metal.

She tugged. The stone was reluctant, and at last she took her sword in her teeth and put both hands to the lifting. Even then it taxed the limit of her strength, and she was strong as many men. But at last it rose, with the strangest sighing sound, and a little prickle of goose-flesh rippled over her.

Now she took the sword back into her hand and knelt on the rim of the invisible blackness below. She had gone this path once before and once only, and never thought to find any necessity in life strong enough to drive her down again. The way was the strangest she had ever known. There was, she thought, no such passage in all the world save here. It had not been built for human feet to travel. It had not been built for feet at all. It was a narrow, polished shaft that cork-screwed round and round. A snake might have slipped in it and gone shooting down, round and round in dizzy circles—but no snake on earth was big enough to fill that shaft. No human travelers had worn the sides of the spiral so smooth, and she did not care to speculate on what creatures had polished it so, through what ages of passage.

She might never have made that first trip down, nor anyone after her, had not some unknown human hacked the notches which made it possible to descend slowly; that is, she thought it must have been a human. At any rate, the notches were roughly shaped for hands and feet, and spaced not too far apart; but who and when and how she could not even guess. As to the beings who made the shaft, in long-forgotten ages—well, there were devils on earth before man, and the world was very old.

She turned on her face and slid feet-first into the curving tunnel. That first time she and Gervase had gone down in sweating terror of what lay below, and with devils tugging at their heels. Now she slid easily, not bothering to find toe-holds, but slipping swiftly round and round the long spirals with only her hands to break the speed when she went too fast. Round and round she went, round and round.

It was a long way down. Before she had gone very far the curious dizziness she had known before came over her again, a dizziness not entirely induced by the spirals she whirled around, but a deeper, atomic unsteadiness as if not only she but also the substances around her were shifting. There was something queer about the angles of those curves. She was no scholar in geometry or aught else, but she felt intuitively that the bend and slant of the way she went were somehow outside any other angles or bends she had ever known. They led into the unknown and the dark, but it seemed to her obscurely that they led into deeper darkness and mystery than the merely physical, as if, though she could not put it clearly even into thoughts, the peculiar and exact lines of the tunnel had been carefully angled to lead through poly-dimensional space as well as through the underground—perhaps through time, too. She did not know she was thinking such things; but all about her was a blurred dizziness as she shot down and round, and she knew that the way she went took her on a stranger journey than any other way she had ever traveled.

Down and down. She was sliding fast, but she knew how long it would be. On that first trip they had taken alarm as the passage spiraled so endlessly and with thoughts of the long climb back had tried to stop before it was too late. They had found it impossible. Once embarked, there was no halting. She had tried, and such waves of sick blurring had come over her that she came near to unconsciousness. It was as if she had tried to halt some inexorable process of nature, half finished. They could only go on. The very atoms of their bodies shrieked in rebellion against a reversal of the change.

And the way up, when they returned, had not been difficult. They had had visions of a back-breaking climb up interminable curves, but again the uncanny difference of those angles from those they knew was manifested. In a queer way they seemed to defy gravity, or perhaps led through some way outside the power of it. They had been sick and dizzy on the return, as on the way down, but through the clouds of that confusion it had seemed to them that they slipped as easily up the shaft as they had gone down; or perhaps that, once in the tunnel, there was neither up nor down.

The passage leveled gradually. This was the worst

part for a human to travel, though it must have eased the speed of whatever beings the shaft was made for. It was too narrow for her to turn in, and she had to lever herself face down and feet first, along the horizontal smoothness of the floor, pushing with her hands. She was glad when her questing heels met open space and she slid from the mouth of the shaft and stood upright in the dark.

Here she paused to collect herself. Yes, this was the beginning of the long passage she and Father Gervase had traveled on that long-ago journey of exploration. By the veriest accident they had found the place, and only the veriest bravado had brought them thus far. He had gone on a greater distance than she—she was younger then, and more amenable to authority—and had come back white-faced in the torchlight and hurried her up the shaft again.

She went on carefully, feeling her way, remembering what she herself had seen in the darkness a little farther on, wondering in spite of herself, and with a tiny catch at her heart, what it was that had sent Father Gervase so hastily back. She had never been entirely satisfied with his explanations. It had been about here—or was it a little farther on? The stillness was like a roaring in her ears.

Then ahead of her the darkness moved. It was just that—a vast, imponderable shifting of the solid dark. Jesu! This was new! She gripped the cross at her throat with one hand and her sword-hilt with the other. Then it was upon her, striking like a hurricane, whirling her against the walls and shrieking in her ears like a thousand wind-devils—a wild cyclone of the dark that buffeted her mercilessly and tore at her flying hair and raved in her ears with the myriad voices of all lost things crying in the night. The voices were piteous in their terror and loneliness. Tears came to her eyes even as she shivered with nameless dread, for the whirlwind was alive with a dreadful instinct, an animate thing sweeping through the dark of the underground; an unholy thing that made her flesh crawl even though it touched her to the heart with its pitiful little lost voices wailing in the wind where no wind could possibly be.

And then it was gone. In that one flash of an instant it vanished, leaving no whisper to commemorate its passage. Only in the heart of it could one hear the sad little voices wailing or the wild shriek of the wind. She found herself standing stunned, her sword yet gripped futilely in one hand and the tears running down her face. Poor little lost voices, wailing. She wiped the tears away with a shaking hand and set her teeth hard against the weakness of reaction that flooded her. Yet it was a good five minutes before she could force herself on. After a few steps her knees ceased to tremble.

The floor was dry and smooth underfoot. It sloped a little downward, and she wondered into what unplumbed deeps she had descended by now. The silence had fallen heavily again, and she found herself straining for some other sound than the soft padding of her own boots. Then her foot slipped in sudden wetness. She bent, exploring fingers outstretched, feeling without reason that the wetness would be red if she could see it. But her fingers traced the immense outline of a footprint—splayed and three-toed like a frog's, but of monster size. It was a fresh footprint. She had a vivid flash of memory—that thing she had glimpsed in the torchlight on the other trip down. But she had light then, and now she was blind in the dark, the creature's natural habitat. . . .

For a moment she was not Jirel of Joiry, vengeful fury on the trail of a devilish weapon, but a frightened woman alone in the unholy dark. That memory had been so vivid. . . . Then she saw Guillaume's scornful, laughing face again, the little beard dark along the line of his jaw, the strong teeth white with his laughter; and something hot and sustaining swept over her like a thin flame, and she was Joiry again, vengeful and resolute. She went on more slowly, her sword swinging in a semicircle before every third step, that she might not be surprised too suddenly by some nightmare monster clasping her in smothering arms. But the flesh crept upon her unprotected back.

The smooth passage went on and on. She could feel the cold walls on either hand, and her upswung sword grazed the roof. It was like crawling through some worm's tunnel, blindly under the weight of countless tons of earth. She felt the pressure of it above and about her, overwhelming, and found herself praying that the end of this tunnel-crawling might come soon, whatever the end might bring.

But when it came it was a stranger thing than she had ever dreamed. Abruptly she felt the immense, imponderable oppression cease. No longer was she conscious of the tons of earth pressing about her. The walls had fallen away and her feet struck a sudden rubble instead of the smooth floor. But the darkness that had bandaged her eyes was changed too, indescribably. It was no longer darkness, but void; not an absence of light, but simple nothingness. Abysses opened around her, yet she could see nothing. She only knew that she stood at the threshold of some immense space, and sensed nameless things about her, and battled vainly against that nothingness which was all her straining eyes could see. And at her throat something constricted painfully.

She lifted her hand and found the chain of her crucifix taut and vibrant around her neck. At that she smiled a little grimly, for she began to understand. The crucifix. She found her hand shaking despite herself, but she unfastened the chain and dropped the cross to the ground. Then she gasped.

All about her, as suddenly as the awakening from a dream, the nothingness had opened out into undreamed-of distances. She stood high on a hilltop under a sky spangled with strange stars. Below she caught glimpses of misty plains and valleys with mountain peaks rising far away. And at her feet a ravening circle of small, slavering, blind things leaped with clashing teeth.

They were obscene and hard to distinguish against the darkness of the hillside, and the noise they made was revolting. Her sword swung up of itself, almost, and slashed furiously at the little dark horrors leaping up around her legs. They died squashily, splattering her bare thighs with unpleasantness, and after a few had gone silent under the blade the rest fled into the dark with quick, frightened pantings, their feet making a queer splashing noise on the stones.

Jirel gathered a handful of the coarse grass which grew there and wiped her legs of the obscene splatters, looking about with quickened breath upon this land so unholy that one who bore a cross might not even see it. Here, if anywhere, one might find a weapon such as she sought. Behind her in the hillside was the low tunnel opening from which she had emerged. Overhead the strange stars shone. She did not recognize a single constellation, and if the brighter sparks were planets they were strange ones, tinged with violet and green and yellow. One was vividly crimson, like a point of fire. Far out over the rolling land below she could discern a mighty column of light. It did not blaze, nor illuminate the dark about it. It cast no shadows. It simply was a great pillar of luminance towering high in the night. It seemed artificial—perhaps man-made, though she scarcely dared hope for men here.

She half expected, despite her brave words, to come out upon the storied and familiar red-hot pave of hell, and this pleasant, starlit land surprised her and made her more wary. The things that built the tunnel could not have been human. She had no right to expect men here. She was a little stunned by finding open sky so far underground, though she was intelligent enough to realize that however she had come, she was not underground now. No cavity in the earth could contain this starry sky. She came of a credulous age, and she accepted her surroundings without too much questioning, though she was a little disappointed, if the truth were known, in the pleasantness of the mistily starlit place. The fiery streets of hell would have been a likelier locality in which to find a weapon against Guillaume.

When she had cleansed her sword on the grass and wiped her legs clean, she turned slowly down the hill. The distant column beckoned her, and after a moment of indecision she turned toward it. She had no time to waste, and this was the likeliest place to find what she sought.

The coarse grass brushed her legs and whispered round her feet. She stumbled now and then on the rubble, for the hill was steep, but she reached the bottom without mishap, and struck out across the meadows toward that blaze of far-away brilliance. It seemed to her that she walked more lightly, somehow. The grass scarcely bent underfoot, and she found she could take long sailing strides like one who runs with wings on his heels. It felt like a dream. The gravity pull of the place must have been less than she was accustomed to, but she only knew that she was skimming over the ground with amazing speed.

Traveling so, she passed through the meadows over the strange, coarse grass, over a brook or two that spoke endlessly to itself in a curious language that was almost speech, certainly not the usual gurgle of earth's running water. Once she ran into a blotch of darkness, like some pocket or void in the air, and struggled through gasping and blinking outraged eyes. She was beginning to realize that the land was not so innocently normal as it looked.

On and on she went, at that surprising speed, while the meadows skimmed past beneath her flying feet and gradually the light drew nearer. She saw now that it was a round tower of sheeted luminance, as if walls of solid flame rose up from the ground. Yet it seemed to be steady, nor did it cast any illumination upon the sky.

Before much time had elapsed, with her dream-like speed she had almost reached her goal. The ground was becoming marshy underfoot, and presently the smell of swamps rose in her nostrils and she saw that between her and the light stretched a belt of unstable ground tufted with black reedy grass. Here and there she could see dim white blotches moving. They might be beasts, or only wisps of mist. The starlight was not very illuminating.

She began to pick her way carefully across the black, quaking morasses. Where the tufts of grass rose she found firmer ground, and she leaped from clump to clump with that amazing lightness, so that her feet barely touched the black ooze. Here and there slow bubbles rose through the mud and broke thickly. She did not like the place.

Half-way across, she saw one of the white blotches approaching her with slow, erratic movements. It bumped along unevenly, and at first she thought it might be inanimate, its approach was so indirect and purposeless. Then it blundered nearer, with that queer bumpy gait, making sucking noises in the ooze and splashing as it came. In the starlight she saw suddenly what it was, and for an instant her heart paused and sickness rose overwhelmingly in her throat. It was a woman—a beautiful woman whose white bare body had the curves and loveliness of some marble statue. She was crouching like a frog, and as Jirel watched in stupefaction she straightened her legs abruptly and leaped as a frog leaps, only more clumsily, falling forward into the ooze a little distance beyond the watching woman. She did not seem to see Jirel. The mud-spattered face was blank. She blundered on through the mud in awkward leaps. Jirel watched until the woman was no more than a white wandering blur in the dark, and above the shock of that sight pity was rising, and uncomprehending resentment against whatever had brought so lovely a creature into this—into blundering in frog leaps aimlessly through the mud, with empty mind and blind, staring eyes. For the second time that night she knew the sting of unaccustomed tears as she went on.

The sight, though, had given her reassurance. The human form was not unknown here. There might be leathery devils with hoofs and horns, such as she still half expected, but she would not be alone in her humanity; though if all the rest were as piteously mindless as the one she had seen—she did not follow that thought. It was too unpleasant. She was glad when the marsh was past and she need not see any longer the awkward white shapes bumping along through the dark.

She struck out across the narrow space which lay between her and the tower. She saw now that it was a building, and that the light composed it. She could not understand that, but she saw it. Walls and columns outlined the tower, solid sheets of light with definite boundaries, not radiant. As she came nearer she saw that it was in motion, apparently spurting up from some source underground as if the light illuminated sheets of water rushing upward under great pressure. Yet she felt intuitively that it was not water, but incarnate light.

She came forward hesitantly, gripping her sword. The area around the tremendous pillar was paved with something black and smooth that did not reflect the light. Out of it sprang the uprushing walls of brilliance with their sharply defined edges. The magnitude of the thing dwarfed her to infinitesimal size. She stared upward with undazzled eyes, trying to understand. If there could be such a thing as solid, no-radiating light, this was it.

IV

She was very near under the mighty tower before she could see the details of the building clearly. They were strange to her—great pillars and arches around the base, and one stupendous portal, all molded out of the rushing, prisoned light. She turned toward the opening after a moment, for the light had a tangible look. She did not believe she could have walked through it even had she dared.

When that tremendous portal arched over her she peered in, affrighted by the very size of the place. She thought she could hear the hiss and spurt of the light surging upward. She was looking into a mighty globe inside, a hall shaped like the interior of a bubble, though the curve was so vast she was scarcely aware of it. And in the very center of the globe floated a light. Jirel blinked. A light, dwelling in a bubble of light. It glowed there in midair with a pale, steady flame that was somehow alive and animate, and brighter than the serene illumination of the building, for it hurt her eyes to look at it directly.

She stood on the threshold and stared, not quite daring to venture in. And as she hesitated a change came over the light. A flash of rose tinged its pallor. The rose deepened and darkened until it took on the color of blood. And the shape underwent strange changes. It lengthened, drew itself out narrowly, split at the bottom into two branches, put out two tendrils from the top. The blood-red paled again, and the light somehow lost its brilliance, receded into the depths of the thing that was forming. Jirel clutched her sword and forgot to breathe, watching. The light was taking on the shape of a human being—of a woman—of a tall woman in mail, her red hair tousled and her eyes staring straight into the duplicate eyes at the portal. . . .

"Welcome," said the Jirel suspended in the center of the globe, her voice deep and resonant and clear in spite of the distance between them. Jirel at the door held her breath, wondering and afraid. This was herself, in every detail, a mirrored Jirel—that was it, a Jirel mirrored upon a surface which blazed and smoldered with barely repressed light, so that the eyes gleamed with it and the whole figure seemed to hold its shape by an effort, only by that effort restraining itself from resolving into pure, formless light again. But the voice was not her own. It shook and resounded with a knowledge as alien as the light-built walls. It mocked her. It said:

"Welcome! Enter into the portals, woman!"

She looked up warily at the rushing walls about her. Instinctively she drew back.

"Enter, enter!" urged the mocking voice from her own mirrored lips. And there was a note in it she did not like.

"Enter!" cried the voice again, this time a command.

Jirel's eyes narrowed. Something intuitive warned her back, and yet—she drew the dagger she had thrust in her belt and with a quick motion she tossed it into the great globe-shaped hall. It struck the floor without a sound, and a brilliant light flared up around it, so brilliant she could not look upon what was happening; but it seemed to her that the knife expanded, grew large and nebulous and ringed with dazzling light. In less time than it takes to tell, it had faded out of sight as if the very atoms which composed it had flown apart and dispersed in the golden glow of that mighty bubble. The dazzle faded with the knife, leaving Jirel staring dazedly at a bare floor.

That other Jirel laughed, a rich, resonant laugh of scorn and malice.

"Stay out, then," said the voice. "You've more intelligence than I thought. Well, what would you here?"

Jirel found her voice with an effort.

"I seek a weapon," she said, "a weapon against a man I so hate that upon earth there is none terrible enough for my need."

"You so hate him, eh?" mused the voice.

"With all my heart!"

"With all your heart!" echoed the voice, and there was an undernote of laughter in it that she did not understand. The echoes of that mirth ran round and round the great globe. Jirel felt her cheeks burn with resentment against some implication in the derision which she could not put a name to. When the echoes of the laugh had faded the voice said indifferently:

"Give the man what you find at the black temple in the lake. I make you a gift of it."

The lips that were Jirel's twisted into a laugh of purest mockery; then all about that figure so perfectly her own the light flared out. She saw the outlines melting fluidly as she turned her dazzled eyes away. Before the echoes of that derision had died, a blinding, formless light burned once more in the midst of the bubble.

Jirel turned and stumbled away under the mighty column of the tower, a hand to her dazzled eyes. Not until she had reached the edge of the black, unreflecting circle that paved the ground around the pillar did she realize that she knew no way of finding the lake where her weapon lay. And not until then did she remember how fatal it is said to be to accept a gift from a demon. Buy it, or earn it, but never accept the gift. Well—she shrugged and stepped out upon the grass. She must surely be damned by now, for having ventured down of her own will into this curious place for such a purpose as hers. The soul can be lost but once.

She turned her face up to the strange stars and wondered in what direction her course lay. The sky looked blankly down upon her with its myriad meaningless eyes. A star fell as she watched, and in her superstitious soul she took it for an omen, and set off boldly over the dark meadows in the direction where the bright streak had faded. No swamps guarded the way here, and she was soon skimming along over the grass with that strange, dancing gait that the lightness of the place allowed her. And as she went she was remembering, as from long ago in some other far world, a man's arrogant mirth and the press of his mouth on hers. Hatred bubbled up hotly within her and broke from her lips in a little savage laugh of anticipation. What dreadful thing awaited her in the temple in the lake, what punishment from hell to be loosed by her own hands upon Guillaume? And though her soul was the price it cost her, she would count it a fair bargain if she could drive that laughter from his mouth and bring terror into the eyes that mocked her.

Thoughts like these kept her company for a long way upon her journey. She did not think to be lonely or afraid in the uncanny darkness across which no shadows fell from that mighty column behind her. The unchanging meadows flew past underfoot, lightly as meadows in a dream. It might almost have been that the earth moved instead of herself, so effortlessly did she go. She was sure now that she was heading in the right direction, for two more stars had fallen in the same arc across the sky.

The meadows were not untenanted. Sometimes she felt presences near her in the dark, and once she ran full-tilt into a nest of little yapping horrors like those on the hill-top. They lunged up about her with clicking teeth, mad with a blind ferocity, and she swung her sword in frantic circles, sickened by the noise of them lunging splashily through the grass and splattering her sword with their deaths. She beat them off and went on, fighting her own sickness, for she had never known anything quite so nauseating as these little monstrosities.

She crossed a brook that talked to itself in the darkness with that queer murmuring which came so near to speech, and a few strides beyond it she paused suddenly, feeling the ground tremble with the rolling thunder of hoofbeats approaching. She stood still, searching the dark anxiously, and presently the earth-shaking beat grew louder and she saw a white blur flung wide across the dimness to her left, and the sound of hoofs deepened and grew. Then out of the night swept a herd of snow-white horses. Magnificently they ran, manes tossing, tails streaming, feet pounding a rhythmic, heart-stirring roll along the ground. She caught her breath at the beauty of their motion. They swept by a little distance away, tossing their heads, spurning the ground with scornful feet.

But as they came abreast of her she saw one blunder and stumble against the next, and that one shook his head bewilderedly; and suddenly she realized that they were blind—all running so splendidly in a deeper dark than even she groped through. And she saw too their coats were roughened with sweat, and foam dripped from their lips, and their nostrils were flaring pools of scarlet. Now and again one stumbled from pure exhaustion. Yet they ran, frantically, blindly through the dark, driven by something outside their comprehension.

As the last one of all swept by her, sweat-crusted and staggering, she saw him toss his head high, spattering foam, and whinny shrilly to the stars. And it seemed to her that the sound was strangely articulate. Almost she heard the echoes of a name—''Julienne! Julienne!''— in that high, despairing sound. And the incongruity of it, the bitter despair, clutched at her heart so sharply that for the third time that night she knew the sting of tears.

The dreadful humanity of that cry echoed in her ears as the thunder died away. She went on, blinking back the tears for that beautiful blind creature, staggering with exhaustion, calling a girl's name hopelessly from a beast's throat into the blank darkness wherein it was for ever lost.

Then another star fell across the sky, and she hurried ahead, closing her mind to the strange, incomprehensible pathos that made an undernote of tears to the starry dark of this land. And the thought was growing in her mind that, though she had come into no brimstone pit where horned devils pranced over flames, yet perhaps it was after all a sort of hell through which she ran.

Presently in the distance she caught a glimmer of

something bright. The ground dipped after that and she lost it, and skimmed through a hollow where pale things wavered away from her into the deeper dark. She never knew what they were, and was glad. When she came up onto higher ground again she saw it more clearly, an expanse of dim brilliance ahead. She hoped it was a lake, and ran more swiftly.

It *was* a lake—a lake that could never have existed outside some obscure hell like this. She stood on the brink doubtfully, wondering if this could be the place the light-devil had meant. Black, shining water stretched out before her, heaving gently with a motion unlike that of any water she had ever seen before. And in the depths of it, like fireflies caught in ice, gleamed myriad small lights. They were fixed there immovably, not stirring with the motion of the water. As she watched, something hissed above her and a streak of light split the dark air. She looked up in time to see something bright curving across the sky to fall without a splash into the water, and small ripples of phosphorescence spread sluggishly toward the shore, where they broke at her feet with the queerest whispering sound, as if each succeeding ripple spoke the syllable of a word.

She looked up, trying to locate the origin of the falling lights, but the strange stars looked down upon her blankly. She bent and stared down into the center of the spreading ripples, and where the thing had fallen she thought a new light twinkled through the water. She could not determine what it was, and after a curious moment she gave the question up and began to cast about for the temple the light-devil had spoken of.

After a moment she thought she saw something dark in the center of the lake, and when she had stared for a few minutes it gradually became clearer, an arch of darkness against the starry background of the water. It might be a temple. She strolled slowly along the brim of the lake, trying to get a closer view of it, for the thing was no more than a darkness against the spangles of light, like some void in the sky where no stars shine. And presently she stumbled over something in the grass.

She looked down with startled yellow eyes, and saw a strange, indistinguishable darkness. It had solidity to the feel but scarcely to the eye, for she could not quite focus upon it. It was like trying to see something that did not exist save as a void, a darkness in the grass. It had the shape of a step, and when she followed with her eyes she saw that it was the beginning of a dim bridge stretching out over the lake, narrow and curved and made out of nothingness. It seemed to have no surface, and its edges were difficult to distinguish from the lesser gloom surrounding it. But the thing was tangible—an arch carved out of the solid dark—and it led out in the direction she wished to go. For she was naïvely sure now that the dim blot in the center of the lake was the temple she was searching for. The falling stars had guided her, and she could not have gone astray.

So she set her teeth and gripped her sword and put her foot upon the bridge. It was rock-firm under her, but scarcely more than a foot or so wide, and without rails. When she had gone a step or two she began to feel dizzy; for under her the water heaved with a motion that made her head swim, and the stars twinkled eerily in its depths. She dared not look away for fear of missing her footing on the narrow arch of darkness. It was like walking a bridge flung across the void, with stars underfoot and nothing but an unstable strip of nothingness to bear her up. Half-way across, the heaving of the water and the illusion of vast, constellated spaces beneath and the look her bridge had of being no more than empty space ahead, combined to send her head reeling; and as she stumbled on, the bridge seemed to be wavering with her, swinging in gigantic arcs across the starry void below.

Now she could see the temple more closely, though scarcely more clearly than from the shore. It looked to be no more than an outlined emptiness against the star-crowded brilliance behind it, etching its arches and columns of blankness upon the twinkling waters. The bridge came down in a long dim swoop to its doorway. Jirel took the last few yards at a reckless run and stopped breathless under the arch that made the temple's vague doorway. She stood there panting and staring about narroweyed, sword poised in her hand. For though the place was empty and very still she felt a presence even as she set her foot upon the floor of it.

She was staring about a little space of blankness in the starry lake. It seemed to be no more than that. She could see the walls and columns where they were outlined against the water and where they made darknesses in the star-flecked sky, but where there was only dark behind them she could see nothing. It was a tiny place, no more than a few square yards of emptiness upon the face of the twinkling waters. And in its center an image stood.

She stared at it in silence, feeling a curious compulsion growing within her, like a vague command from something outside herself. The image was of some substance of nameless black, unlike the material which composed the building, for even in the dark she could see it clearly. It was a semi-human figure, crouching forward with outthrust head, sexless and strange. Its one central eye was closed as if in rapture, and its mouth was pursed for a kiss. And though it was but an image and without even the semblance of life, she felt unmistakably the presence of something alive in the temple, something so alien and innominate that instinctively she drew away.

She stood there for a full minute, reluctant to enter the place where so alien a being dwelt, half conscious of that voiceless compulsion growing up within her. And slowly she became aware that all the lines and angles of the halfseen building were curved to make the image their center and focus. The very bridge swooped its long arc to complete the centering. As she watched, it seemed to her that through the arches of the columns even the stars in lake and sky were grouped in patterns which took the image for their focus. Every line and curve in the dim world seemed to sweep round toward the squatting thing before her with its closed eye and expectant mouth.

Gradually the universal focusing of lines began to exert its influence upon her. She took a hesitant step forward without realizing the motion. But that step was all the dormant urge within her needed. With her one motion forward the compulsion closed down upon her with whirlwind impetuosity. Helplessly she felt herself advancing, helplessly with one small, sane portion of her mind she realized the madness that was gripping her, the blind, irresistible urge to do what every visible

line in the temple's construction was made to compel.
With stars swirling around her she advanced across the
floor and laid her hands upon the rounded shoulders of
the image—the sword, forgotten, making a sort of
accolade against its hunched neck—and lifted her red
head and laid her mouth blindly against the pursed lips
of the image.

In a dream she took that kiss. In a dream of dizziness
and confusion she seemed to feel the iron-cold lips
stirring under hers. And through the union of that
kiss—warm-blooded woman with image of nameless
stone—through the meeting of their mouths something
entered into her very soul; something cold and stunning; something alien beyond any words. It lay upon
her shuddering soul like some frigid weight from the
void, a bubble holding something unthinkably alien and
dreadful. She could feel the heaviness of it upon some
intangible part of her that shrank from the touch. It was
like the weight of remorse or despair, only far colder
and stranger and—somehow—more ominous, as if this
weight were but the egg from which things might hatch
too dreadful to put even into thoughts.

The moment of the kiss could have been no longer
than a breath's space, but to her it was timeless. In a
dream she felt the compulsion falling from her at last. In
a dim dream she dropped her hands from its shoulders,
finding the sword heavy in her grasp and staring dully at
it for a while before clarity began its return to her cloudy
mind. When she became completely aware of herself
once more she was standing with slack body and dragging head before the blind, rapturous image, that dead
weight upon her heart as dreary as an old sorrow, and

more coldly ominous than anything she could find words for.

And with returning clarity the most staggering terror came over her, swiftly and suddenly—terror of the image and the temple of darkness, and the coldly spangled lake and of the whole, wide, dim, dreadful world about her. Desperately she longed for home again, even the red fury of hatred and the press of Guillaume's mouth and the hot arrogance of his eyes again. Anything but this. She found herself running without knowing why. Her feet skimmed over the narrow bridge lightly as a gull's wings dipping the water. In a brief instant the starry void of the lake flashed by beneath her and the solid earth was underfoot. She saw the great column of light far away across the dark meadows and beyond it a hill-top rising against the stars. And she ran.

She ran with terror at her heels and devils howling in the wind her own speed made. She ran from her own curiously alien body, heavy with its weight of inexplicable doom. She passed through the hollow where pale things wavered away, she fled over the uneven meadows in a frenzy of terror. She ran and ran, in those long light bounds the lesser gravity allowed her, fleeter than a deer, and her own panic choked in her throat and that weight upon her soul dragged at her too drearily for tears. She fled to escape it, and could not; and the ominous certainty that she carried something too dreadful to think of grew and grew.

For a long while she skimmed over the grass tirelessly, wing-heeled, her red hair flying. The panic died after a while, but that sense of heavy disaster did not die. She felt somehow that tears would ease her, but something in the frigid darkness of her soul froze her tears in the ice of that gray and alien chill.

And gradually, through the inner dark, a fierce anticipation took form in her mind. Revenge upon Guillaume! She had taken from the temple only a kiss, so it was that which she must deliver to him. And savagely she exulted in the thought of what that kiss would release upon him, unsuspecting. She did not know, but it filled her with fierce joy to guess.

She had passed the column and skirted the morass where the white, blundering forms still bumped along awkwardly through the ooze, and was crossing the coarse grass toward the nearing hill when the sky began to pale along the horizon. And with that pallor a fresh terror took hold upon her, a wild horror of daylight in this unholy land. She was not sure if it was the light itself she so dreaded, or what that light would reveal in the dark stretches she had traversed so blindly—what unknown horrors she had skirted in the night. But she knew instinctively that if she valued her sanity she must be gone before the light had risen over the land. And she redoubled her efforts, spurring her wearying limbs to yet more skimming speed. But it would be a lose race, for already the stars were blurring out, and a flush of curious green was broadening along the sky, and around her the air was turning to a vague, unpleasant gray.

She toiled up the steep hillside breathlessly. When she was half-way up, her own shadow began to take form upon the rocks, and it was unfamiliar and dreadfully significant of something just outside her range of understanding. She averted her eyes from it, afraid that at any moment the meaning might break upon her outraged brain.

She could see the top of the hill above her, dark against the paling sky, and she toiled up in frantic haste, clutching her sword and feeling that if she had to look in the full light upon the dreadful little abominations that had snapped around her feet when she first emerged she would collapse into screaming hysteria.

The cave-mouth yawned before her, invitingly black, a refuge from the dawning light behind her. She knew an almost irresistible desire to turn and look back from this vantage-point across the land she had traversed, and gripped her sword hard to conquer the perversive longing. There was a scuffling in the rocks at her feet, and she set her teeth in her underlip and swung viciously in brief arcs, without looking down. She heard small squeakings and the splashy sound of feet upon the stones, and felt her blade sheer thrice through semi-solidity, to the click of little vicious teeth. Then they broke and ran off over the hillside, and she stumbled on, choking back the scream that wanted so fiercely to break from her lips.

She fought that growing desire all the way up to the cave-mouth, for she knew that if she gave way she would never cease shrieking until her throat went raw.

Blood was trickling from her bitten lip with the effort at silence when she reached the cave. And there, twinkling upon the stones, lay something small and bright and dearly familiar. With a sob of relief she bent and snatched up the crucifix she had torn from her throat when she came out into this land. And as her fingers shut upon it a vast, protecting darkness swooped around her. Gasping with relief, she groped her way the step or two that separated her from the cave.

Dark lay like a blanket over her eyes, and she welcomed it gladly, remembering how her shadow had lain so awfully upon the hillside as she climbed, remembering the first rays of savage sunlight beating upon her shoulders. She stumbled through the blackness, slowly getting control again over her shaking body and laboring lungs, slowly stilling the panic that the dawning day has roused so inexplicably within her. And as that terror died, the dull weight upon her spirit became strong again. She had all but forgotten it in her panic, but now the impending and unknown dreadfulness grew heavier and more oppressive in the darkness of the underground, and she groped along in a dull stupor of her own depression, slow with the weight of the strange doom she carried.

Nothing barred her way. In the dullness of her stupor she scarcely realized it, or expected any of the vague horrors that peopled the place to leap out upon her. Empty and unmenacing, the way stretched before her blindly stumbling feet. Only once did she hear the sound of another presence—the rasp of hoarse breathing and the scrape of a scaly hide against the stone—but it must have been outside the range of her own passage, for she encountered nothing.

When she had come to the end and a cold wall rose up before her, it was scarcely more than automatic habit that made her search along it with groping hand until she came to the mouth of the shaft. It sloped gently up into the dark. She crawled in, trailing her sword, until the rising incline and lowering roof forced her down upon her face. Then with toes and fingers she began to force herself up the spiral, slippery way.

Before she had gone very far she was advancing without effort, scarcely realizing that it was against gravity she moved. The curious dizziness of the shaft had come over her, the strange feeling of change in the very substance of her body, and through the cloudy numbness of it she felt herself sliding round and round the spirals, without effort. Again, obscurely, she had the feeling that in the peculiar angles of this shaft was neither up nor down. And for a long while the dizzy circling went on.

When the end came at last, and she felt her fingers gripping the edge of that upper opening which lay beneath the floor of Joiry's lowest dungeons, she heaved herself up wearily and lay for awhile on the cold floor in the dark, while slowly the clouds of dizziness passed from her mind, leaving only that ominous weight within. When the darkness had ceased to circle about her, and the floor steadied, she got up dully and swung the cover back over the opening, her hands shuddering from the feel of the cold, smooth ring which had never seen daylight.

When she turned from this task she was aware of the reason for the lessening in the gloom around her. A guttering light outlined the hole in the wall from which she had pulled the stones—was it a century ago? The brilliance all but blinded her after her long sojourn through blackness, and she stood there awhile, swaying a little, one hand to her eyes, before she went out into the familiar torchlight she knew waited her beyond. Father Gervase, she was sure, anxiously waited her return. But even he had not dared to follow her through the hole in the wall, down to the brink of the shaft.

Somehow she felt that she should be giddy with relief at this safe homecoming, back to humanity again. But as she stumbled over the upward slope toward light and safety she was conscious of no more than the dullness of whatever unreleased horror it was which still lay so ominously upon her stunned soul.

She came through the gaping hole in the masonry into the full glare of torches awaiting her, remembering with a wry inward smile how wide she had made the opening in anticipation of flight from something dreadful when she came back that way. Well, there was no flight from the horror she bore within her. It seemed to her that her heart was slowing, too, missing a beat now and then and staggering like a wary runner.

She came out into the torchlight, stumbling with exhaustion, her mouth scarlet from the blood of her bitten lip and her bare greaved legs and bare sword-blade foul with the deaths of those little horrors that swarmed around the cave-mouth. From the tangle of red hair her eyes stared out with a bleak, frozen inward look, as of one who has seen nameless things. That keen, steel-bright beauty which had been hers was as dull and fouled as her sword-blade, and at the look in her eyes Father Gervase shuddered and crossed himself.

V

They were waiting for her in an uneasy group—the priest anxious and dark, Guillaume splendid in the torchlight, tall and arrogant, a handful of men-at-arms holding the guttering lights and shifting uneasily from one foot to the other. When she saw Guillaume the light that flared up in her eyes blotted out for a moment the bleak dreadfulness behind them, and her slowing heart leaped like a spurred horse, sending the blood riotously through her veins. Guillaume, magnificent in his armor, leaning upon his sword and staring down at her from his scornful height, the little black beard jutting. Guillaume, to whom Joiry had fallen. Guillaume.

That which she carried at the core of her being was heavier than anything else in the world, so heavy she could scarcely keep her knees from bending, so heavy her heart labored under its weight. Almost irresistibly she wanted to give way beneath it, to sink down and down under the crushing load, to lie prone and vanquished in the ice-gray, bleak place she was so dimly aware of through the clouds that were rising about her. But there was Guillaume, grim and grinning, and she hated him so very bitterly—she must make the effort. She must, at whatever cost, for she was coming to know that death lay in wait for her if she bore this burden long, that it was a two-edged weapon which could strike at its wielder if the blow were delayed too long. She knew this through the dim mists that were thickening in her brain, and she put all her strength into the immense effort it cost to cross the floor toward him. She stumbled a little, and made one faltering step and then another, and dropped her sword with a clang as she lifted her arms to him.

He caught her strongly, in a hard, warm clasp, and she heard his laugh triumphant and hateful as he bent his head to take the kiss she was raising her mouth to offer. He must have seen, in that last moment before their lips met, the savage glare of victory in her eyes, and been startled. But he did not hesitate. His mouth was heavy upon hers.

It was a long kiss. She felt him stiffen in her arms. She felt a coldness in the lips upon hers, and slowly the dark weight of what she bore lightened, lifted, cleared away from her cloudy mind. Strength flowed back through her richly. The whole world came alive to her once more. Presently she loosed his slack arms and stepped away, looking up into his face with a keen and dreadful triumph upon her own.

She saw the ruddiness of him draining away, and the rigidity of stone coming over his scarred features. Only his eyes remained alive, and there was torment in them, and understanding. She was glad—she had wanted him to understand what it cost to take Joiry's kiss unbidden. She smiled thinly into his tortured eyes, watching. And she saw something cold and alien seeping through him, permeating him slowly with some unnamable emotion which no man could ever have experienced before. She could not name it, but she saw it in his eyes—some dreadful emotion never made for flesh and blood to know, some iron despair such as only an unguessable being from the gray, formless void could ever have felt before—too hideously alien for any human creature to endure. Even she shuddered from the dreadful, cold bleakness looking out of his eyes, and knew as she watched that there must be many emotions and many fears and joys too far outside man's comprehension for any being of flesh to undergo, and live. Grayly she saw it spreading through him, and the very substance of his body shuddered under that iron weight.

And now came a visible, physical change. Watching, she was aghast to think that in her own body and upon her own soul she had borne the seed of this dreadful flowering, and did not wonder that her heart had slowed under the unbearable weight of it. He was standing rigidly with arms half bent, just as he stood when she slid from his embrace. And now great shudders began to go over him, as if he were wavering in the torchlight, some grey-faced wraith in armor with torment in his eyes. She saw the sweat beading his forehead. She saw a trickle of blood from his mouth, as if he had bitten through his lip in the agony of this new, incomprehensible emotion. Then a last shiver went over him violently, and he flung up his head, the little curling beard jutting ceilingward and the muscles of his strong throat corded, and from his lips broke a long, low cry of such utter, inhuman strangeness that Jirel felt coldness rippling through her veins and she put up her hands to her ears to shut it out. It meant something—it expressed some dreadful emotion that was neither sorrow nor despair nor anger, but infinitely alien and infinitely sad. Then his long legs buckled at the knees and he dropped with a clatter of mail and lay still on the stone floor.

They knew he was dead. That was unmistakable in the way he lay. Jirel stood very still, looking down upon him, and strangely it seemed to her that all the lights in the world had gone out. A moment before he had been so big and vital, so magnificent in the torchlight—she could still feel his kiss upon her mouth, and the hard warmth of his arms. . . .

Suddenly and blindingly it came upon her what she had done. She knew now why such heady violence had flooded her whenever she thought of him—knew why the light-devil in her own form had laughed so derisively—knew the price she must pay for taking a gift from a demon. She knew that there was no light anywhere in the world, now that Guillaume was gone.

Father Gervase took her arm gently. She shook him off with an impatient shrug and dropped to one knee beside Guillaume's body, bending her head so that the red hair fell forward to hide her tears.

Black God's Shadow

Through Jirel's dreams a faraway voice went wailing. She opened yellow eyes upon darkness and lay still for a while, wondering what had waked her and staring into the gloom of her tower chamber, listening to the familiar night sounds of the sentry on the battlements close overhead, the rattle of armor and the soft shuffle of feet in the straw laid down to muffle the sound so that Joiry's lady might sleep in peace.

And as she lay there in the dark, quite suddenly the old illusion came over her again. She felt the pressure of strong mailed arms and the weight of a bearded mouth insolently upon hers, and she closed her red lips on an oath at her own weakness and knew again the sting of helpless tears behind her eyelids.

She lay quiet, remembering. Guillaume—so hatefully magnificent in his armor, grinning down upon her from her own dais in her own castle hall where her own dead soldiers lay scattered about upon the bloody flags. Guillaume—his arms hard about her, his mouth heavy upon her own. Even now anger swept like a flame across her memory in answer to the arrogance and scorn of that conqueror's kiss. Yet was it anger?—was it hatred? And how had she to know, until he lay dead at last at her vengeful feet, that it was not hate which bubbled up so hotly whenever she remembered the insolence of his arms, or that he had defeated her men and conquered unconquerable Joiry? For she had been the commander of the strongest fortress in the kingdom, and called no man master, and it was her proudest boast that Joiry would never fall, and that no lover dared lay hands upon her save in answer to her smile.

No, it had not been hatred which answered Guillaume's overwhelming arrogance. Not hate, though the fire and fury of it had gone storming like madness through her. So many loves had blown lightly through her life before—how was she to know this surge of heady violence for what it was, until too late? Well, it was ended now.

She had gone down the secret way that she and one other knew, down into that dark and nameless hell which none who wore a cross might enter, where God's dominion ended at the portals, and who could tell what strange and terrible gods held sway instead? She remembered the starry darkness of it, and the voices that cried along the wind, and the brooding perils she could not understand. No other thing than the flame of her—hatred?—could have driven her down, and nothing but its violence could have sustained her along the dark ways she went seeking a weapon worthy to slay Guillaume.

Well, she had found it. She had taken the black god's kiss. Heavy and cold upon her soul she had carried it back, feeling the terrible weight bearing down upon some intangible part of her that shuddered and shrank from the touch. She had fouled her very soul with that burden, but she had not guessed what terrible potentialities it bore within it, like some egg of hell's spawning to slay the man she loved.

Her weapon was a worthy one. She smiled grimly, remembering that—remembering her return, and how triumphantly he had accepted that kiss from hell, not understanding. . . . Again she saw the awful fruition of her vengeance, as the chill of her soul's burden shifted, through the meeting of their mouths, from her soul to his. Again she saw the spreading of that nameless emotion from Beyond through his shuddering body, an iron despair which no flesh and blood could endure.

Yes, a worthy weapon. She had periled her soul in the seeking of it, and slain him with a god-cursed kiss, and known too late that she would never love another man. Guillaume—tall and splendid in his armor, the little black beard split by the whiteness of his grin, and arrogance sneering from his scarred and scornful face. Guillaume—whose kiss would haunt her all the nights of her life. Guillaume—who was dead. In the dark she hid her face upon her bent arm, and the red hair fell forward to smother her sobs.

When sleep came again she did not know. But presently she was alone in a dim, formless place through whose mists the far-away voice wailed fretfully. It was a familiar voice with strange, plaintive overtones—a sad little lost voice wailing through the dark.

"Oh, Jirel," it moaned reedily, the tiniest thread of sound. "Oh, Jirel—my murderess. . . ."

And in the dream her heart stood still, and—though she had killed more men than one—she thought she knew that voice, tiny and thin though it was in the bodiless dark of her sleep. And she held her breath, listening. It came again, "Oh, Jirel! It is Guillaume calling—Guillaume, whom you slew. Is there no end to your vengeance? Have mercy, oh my murderess! Release my soul from the dark god's torment. Oh Jirel—Jirel—I pray your mercy!"

Jirel awoke wet-eyed and lay there staring into the dark, recalling that pitiful little reedy wail which had once been Guillaume's rich, full-throated voice. And wondering. The dark god? True, Guillaume had died unshriven, with all his sins upon him, and because of this she had supposed that his soul plunged straight downward to the gates of hell.

Yet—could it be? By the power of that infernal kiss which she had braved the strange dark underground to get as a weapon against him—by the utter strangeness of it, and the unhuman death he died, it must be that now his naked soul wandered, lost and lonely, through that nameless hell lit by strange stars, where ghosts moved in curious forms through the dark. And he asked her mercy—Guillaume, who in life had asked mercy of no living creature.

She heard the watch changing on the battlements above, and dropped again into an uneasy slumber, and once more entered the dim place where the little voice cried through the mist, wailing piteously for mercy from her vengeance. Guillaume—the proud Guillaume, with his deep voice and scornful eyes. Guillaume's lost soul wailing through her dreams . . . "Have mercy upon me, oh my murderess!" . . . and again she woke with wet eyes and started up, staring wildly around her in the gloom and thinking that surely she heard yet the echo of the little lost voice crying. And as the sound faded from her ears she knew that she must go down again.

For a while she lay there, shivering a little and forcing herself into the knowledge. Jirel was a brave woman and a savage warrior, and the most reckless soldier of all her men-at-arms. There was not a man for miles about who did not fear and respect Joiry's commander—her sword-keen beauty and her reckless courage and her skill at arms. But at the thought of what she must do to save Guillaume's soul the coldness of terror blew over her and her heart contracted forebodingly. To go down again—down into the perilous, star-lit dark among dangers more dreadful than she could put words to—dared she? Dared she go?

She rose at last, cursing her own weakness. The stars through the narrow windows watched her pull on her doeskin shirt and the brief tunic of linked mail over it. She buckled the greaves of a long-dead Roman legionary on her slim, strong legs, and, as on that unforgettable night not long since when she had dressed for this same journey, she took her two-edged sword unsheathed in her hand.

Again she went down through the dark of the sleeping castle. Joiry's dungeons are deep, and she descended a long way through the oozing, dank corridors underground, past cells where the bones of Joiry's enemies rotted in forgotten chains. And she, who feared no living man, was frightened in that haunted dark, and gripped her sword closer and clutched the cross at her neck with nervous fingers. The silence hurt her ears with its weight, and the dark was like a bandage over her straining eyes.

At the end of the last oozing passage, far underground, she came to a wall. With her free hand she set to work pulling the unmortared stones from their places, making an opening to squeeze through—trying not to remember that upon this spot that dreadful night tall Guillaume had died, with the black god's kiss burning upon his mouth and unnamable torment in his eyes. Here upon these stones. Against the darkness vividly she could see that torch-lit scene, and Guillaume's long mailed body sprawled across the floor. She would never forget that. Perhaps even after she died she would remember the smoky, acrid smell of the torches, and the coldness of the stones under her bare knees as she knelt beside the body of the man she had killed; the choke in her throat, and the brush of the red hair against her cheek, falling forward to mask her tears from the stolid men-at-arms. And Guillaume— Guillaume. . . .

She took her lip between her teeth resolutely, and turned her mind to the pulling out of stones. Presently there was a hole big enough for her slim height, and she pushed through into the solid dark beyond. Her feet were upon a ramp, and she went down cautiously, feeling her way with exploring toes. When the floor leveled she dropped to her knees and felt for the remembered circle in the pavement. She found that, and the curious cold ring in its center, of some nameless metal which daylight had never shone upon, metal so smooth and cold and strange that her fingers shuddered as she gripped it and heaved. That lid was heavy. As before, she had to take her sword in her teeth, for she dared not lay it down, and use both hands to lift the stone circle. It rose with an odd little sighing sound, as if some suction from below had gripped it and were released.

She sat on the edge for a moment, swinging her feet in the opening and gathering all her courage for the plunge. When she dared hesitate no longer, for fear she would never descend if she delayed another instant, she caught her breath and gripped her sword hard and plunged.

It must have been the strangest descent that the world has known—not a shaft but a spiral twisting down in smooth, corkscrew loops, a spiral made for no human creature to travel, yet into whose sides in some forgotten era a nameless human had cut notches for hands and feet, so that Jirel went down more slowly than if she had had to take an unbroken plunge. She slipped smoothly along down the spirals, barely braking her passage now and again by grasping at the notches in the wall when she felt herself sliding too fast.

Presently the familiar sickness came over her—that strange, inner dizziness as if the spiral were taking her not only through space but through dimensions, and the very structure of her body were altering and shifting with the shifting spirals. And it seemed, too, that down any other shaft she would have fallen more swiftly. This was not a free glide downward—she scarcely seemed to be falling at all. In the spiral there was neither up nor down, and the sickness intensified until in the whirling loops and the whirling dizziness she lost all count of time and distance, and slid through the dark in a stupor of her own misery.

*   *   *

At long last the spiral straightened and began to incline less steeply, and she knew that she approached the end. It was hard work then, levering herself along the gentle slope on hands and knees, and when she came out at last into open darkness she scrambled to her feet and stood panting, sword in hand, straining her eyes against the impenetrable dark of this place that must be without counterpart anywhere in the world, or outside it. There were perils here, but she scarcely thought of them as she set out through the dark, for remembering those greater perils beyond.

She went forward warily for all that, swinging her sword in cautious arcs before her that she might not run full-tilt into some invisible horror. It was an unpleasant feeling, this groping through blackness, knowing eyes upon her, feeling presences near her, watching. Twice she heard hoarse breathing, and once the splat of great wet feet upon stone, but nothing touched her or tried to bar her passage.

Nevertheless she was shaking with tension and terror when at last she reached the end of the passage. There was no visible sign to tell her that it was ended, but as before, suddenly she sensed that the oppression of those vast weights of earth on all sides had lifted. She was standing at the threshold of some mighty void. The very darkness had a different quality—and at her throat something constricted.

Jirel gripped her sword a little more firmly and felt for the crucifix at her neck—found it—lifted the chain over her head.

Instantly a burst of blinding radiance smote her dark-accustomed eyes more violently than a blow. She stood at a cave mouth, high on the side of a hill, staring out over the most blazing day she had ever seen. Heat and light shimmered in the dazzle: strangely colored light, heat that danced and shook. Day, over a dreadful land.

Jirel cried out inarticulately and clapped a hand over her outraged eyes, groping backward step by step into the sheltering dark of the cave. Night in this land was terrible enough, but day—no, she dared not look upon the strange hell save when darkness veiled it. She remembered that other journey, when she had raced the dawn up the hillside, shuddering, averting her eyes from the terror of her own misshapen shadow forming upon the stones. No, she must wait, how long she could not guess; for though it had been night above ground when she left, here was broad day, and it might be that day in this land was of a different duration from that she knew.

She drew back farther into the cave, until that dreadful day was no more than a blur upon the darkness, and sat down with her back to the rock and the sword across her bare knees, waiting. That blurred light upon the walls had a curious tinge of color such as she had never seen in any earthly daylight. It seemed to her that it shimmered—paled and deepened and brightened again as if the illumination were not steady. It had almost the quality of firelight in its fluctuations.

Several times something seemed to pass across the cave-mouth, blotting out the light for an instant, and once she saw a great, stooping shadow limned upon the wall, as if something had paused to peer within the cave. And at the thought of what might rove this land by

day Jirel shivered as if in a chill wind, and groped for
her crucifix before she remembered that she no longer
wore it.

She waited for a long while, clasping cold hands
about her knees, watching that blur upon the wall in
fascinated anticipation. After a time she may have
dozed a little, with the light, unresting sleep of one
poised to wake at the tiniest sound or motion. It seemed
to her that eternities went by before the light began to
pale upon the cave wall.

She watched it fading. It did not move across the wall
as sunlight would have done. The blur remained motionless, dimming slowly, losing its tinge of unearthly
color, taking on the blueness of evening. Jirel stood up
and paced back and forth to limber her stiffened body.
But not until that blur had faded so far that no more than
the dimmest glimmer of radiance lay upon the stone did
she venture out again toward the cave-mouth.

Once more she stood upon the hilltop, looking out
over a land lighted by strange constellations that
sprawled across the sky in pictures whose outlines she
could not quite trace, though there was about them a
dreadful familiarity. And, looking up upon the spreading patterns in the sky, she realized afresh that this land,
whatever it might be, was no underground cavern of
whatever vast dimensions. It was open air she breathed,
and stars in a celestial void she gazed upon, and however she had come here, she was no longer under the
earth.

Below her the dim country spread. And it was not the
same landscape she had seen on that other journey. No
mighty column of shadowless light swept skyward in
the distance. She caught the glimmer of a broad river

where no river had flowed before, and the ground here and there was patched and checkered with pale radiance, like luminous fields laid out orderly upon the darkness.

She stepped down the hill delicately, poised for the attack of those tiny, yelping horrors that had raved about her knees once before. They did not come. Surprised, hoping against hope that she was to be spared that nauseating struggle, she went on. The way down was longer than she remembered. Stones turned under her feet, and coarse grass slashed at her knees. She was wondering as she descended where her search was to begin, for in all the dark, shifting land she saw nothing to guide her, and Guillaume's voice was no more than a fading memory from her dream. She could not even find her way back to the lake where the black god crouched, for the whole landscape was changed unrecognizably.

So when, unmolested, she reached the foot of the hill, she set off at random over the dark earth, running as before with that queer dancing lightness, as if the gravity pull of this place were less than that to which she was accustomed, so that the ground seemed to skim past under her flying feet. It was like a dream, this effortless glide through the darkness, fleet as the wind.

Presently she began to near one of those luminous patches that resembled fields, and saw now that they were indeed a sort of garden. The luminosity rose from myriads of tiny, darting lights planted in even rows, and when she came near enough she saw that the lights were small insects, larger than fireflies, and with luminous wings which they beat vainly upon the air, darting from side to side in a futile effort to be free. For each was attached to its little stem, as if they had sprung living from the soil. Row upon row of them stretched into the dark.

She did not even speculate upon who had sowed such seed here, or toward what strange purpose. Her course led her across a corner of the field, and as she ran she broke several of the stems, releasing the shining prisoners. They buzzed up around her instantly, angrily as bees, and wherever a luminous wing brushed her a hot pain stabbed. She beat them off after a while and ran on, skirting other fields with new wariness.

She crossed a brook that spoke to itself in the dark with a queer, whispering sound so near to speech that she paused for an instant to listen, then thought she had caught a word or two of such dreadful meaning that she ran on again, wondering if it could have been only an illusion.

Then a breeze sprang up and brushed the red hair from her ears, and it seemed to her that she caught the faintest, far wailing. She stopped dead-still, listening, and the breeze stopped too. But she was almost certain she had heard that voice again, and after an instant's hesitation she turned in the direction from which the breeze had blown.

It led toward the river. The ground grew rougher, and she began to hear water running with a subdued, rushing noise, and presently again the breeze brushed her face. Once more she thought she could hear the dimmest echo of the voice that had cried in her dreams.

When she came to the brink of the water she paused for a moment, looking down to where the river rushed between steep banks. The water had a subtle difference in appearance from water in the rivers she knew—somehow thicker, for all its swift flowing. When she leaned out to look, her face was mirrored monstrously upon the broken surface, in a way that no earthly water would reflect, and as the image fell upon its torrent the water broke there violently, leaping upward and splashing as if some hidden rock had suddenly risen in its bed. There was a hideous eagerness about it, as if the water were ravening for her, rising in long, hungry leaps against the rocky walls to splash noisily and run back into the river. But each leap came higher against the wall, and Jirel started back in something like alarm, a vague unease rising within her at the thought of what might happen if she waited until the striving water reached high enough.

At her withdrawal the tumult lessened instantly, and after a moment or so she knew by the sound that the river had smoothed over its broken place and was flowing on undisturbed. Shivering a little, she went on upstream whence the fitful breeze seemed to blow.

Once she stumbled into a patch of utter darkness and fought through in panic fear of walking into the river in her blindness, but she won free of the curious air-pocket without mishap. And once the ground under her skimming feet quaked like jelly, so that she could scarcely keep her balance as she fled on over the unstable section. But ever the little breeze blew and died away and blew again, and she thought the faint echo of a cry was becoming clearer. Almost she caught the far-away sound of ''Jirel—'' moaning upon the wind, and quickened her pace.

For some while now she had been noticing a growing

pallor upon the horizon, and wondering uneasily if night could be so short here, and day already about to dawn. But no—for she remembered that upon that other terrible dawn which she had fled so fast to escape, the pallor had ringed the whole horizon equally, as if day rose in one vast circle clear around the nameless land. Now it was only one spot on the edge of the sky which showed that unpleasant, dawning light. It was faintly tinged with green that strengthened as she watched, and presently above the hills in the distance rose the rim of a vast green moon. The stars paled around it. A cloud floated across its face, writhed for an instant as if in some skyey agony, then puffed into a mist and vanished, leaving the green face clear again.

And it was a mottled face across which dim things moved very slowly. Almost it might have had an atmosphere of its own, and dark clouds floating sluggishly; and if that were so it must have been self-luminous, for these slow masses dimmed its surface and it cast little light despite its hugeness. But there was light enough so that in the land through which Jirel ran great shadows took shape upon the ground, writhing and shifting as the moon-clouds obscured and revealed the green surface, and the whole night scene was more baffling and unreal than a dream. And there was something about the green luminance that made her eyes ache.

She waded through shadows as she ran now, monstrous shadows with a hideous dissimilarity to the things that cast them, and no two alike, however identical the bodies which gave them shape. Her own shadow, keeping pace with her along the ground, she did not look at after one shuddering glance. There was something so unnatural about it, and yet—yet it was like her, too, with a dreadful likeness she could not fathom. And more than once she saw great shadows drifting across the ground without any visible thing to cast them—nothing but the queerly shaped blurs moving soundlessly past her and melting into the farther dark. And that was the worst of all.

She ran on upwind, ears straining for a repetition of the far crying, skirting the shadows as well as she could and shuddering whenever a great dark blot drifted noiselessly across her path. The moon rose slowly up the sky, tinting the night with a livid greenness, bringing it dreadfully to life with moving shadows. Sometimes the sluggishly moving darknesses across its face clotted together and obscured the whole great disk, and she ran on a few steps thankfully through the unlighted dark before the moon-clouds parted again and the dead green face looked blankly down once more, the cloud-masses crawling across it like corruption across a corpse's face.

During one of these darknesses something slashed viciously at her leg, and she heard the grate of teeth on the greave she wore. When the moon unveiled again she saw a long bright scar along the metal, and a drip of phosphorescent venom trickling down. She gathered a handful of grass to wipe it off before it reached her unprotected foot, and the grass withered in her hand when the poison touched it.

All this while the river had been rushing past her and away, and as she ran it began to narrow and diminish; so she knew she must be approaching its head. When the wind blew she was sure now that she heard her own name upon it, in the small wail which had once been

Guillaume's scornful voice. Then the ground began to rise, and down the hillside she mounted, the river fell tinkling, a little thread of water no larger than a brook.

The tinkling was all but articulate now. The river's rush had been no more than a roaring threat, but the voice of the brook was deliberately clear, a series of small, bright notes like syllables, saying evil things. She tried not to listen, for fear of understanding.

The hill rose steeper, and the brook's voice sharpened and clarified and sang delicately in its silvery poisonous tones, and above her against the stars she presently began to discern something looming on the very height of the hill, something like a hulking figure motionless as the hill it crowned. She gripped her sword and slackened her pace a little, skirting the dark thing warily. But when she came near enough to make it out in the green moonlight she saw that it was no more than an image crouching there, black as darkness, giving back a dull gleam from its surface where the lividness of the moon struck it. Its shadow moved uneasily upon the ground.

The guiding wind had fallen utterly still now. She stood in a breathless silence before the image, and the stars sprawled their queer patterns across the sky and the sullen moonlight poured down upon her and nothing moved anywhere but those quivering shadows that were never still.

The image had the shape of a black, shambling thing with shallow head sunk between its shoulders and great arms dragging forward on the ground. But something about it, something indefinable and obscene, reminded her of Guillaume. Some aptness of line and angle parodied in the ugly hulk the long, clean lines of Guillaume, the poise of his high head, the scornful tilt of his chin. She could not put a finger on any definite likeness, but it was unmistakably there. And it was all the ugliness of Guillaume—she saw it as she stared. All his cruelty and arrogance and brutish force. The image might have been a picture of Guillaume's sins, with just enough of his virtues left in to point its dreadfulness.

For an instant she thought she could see behind the black parody, rising from it and irrevocably part of it, a nebulous outline of the Guillaume she had never known, the scornful face twisted in despair, the splendid body writhing futilely away from that obscene thing which was himself—Guillaume's soul, rooted in the ugliness which the image personified. And she knew his punishment—so just, yet so infinitely unjust.

And what subtle torment the black god's kiss had wrought upon him! To dwell in the full, frightful realization of his own sins, chained to the actual manifestation, suffering eternally in the obscene shape that was so undeniably himself—his worst and lowest self. It was just, in a way. He had been a harsh and cruel man in life. But the very fact that such punishment was agony to him proved a higher self within his complex soul—something noble and fine which writhed away from the unspeakable thing—himself. So the very fineness of him was a weapon to torture his soul, turned against him even as his sins were turned.

She understood all this in the timeless moment while she stood there with eyes fixed motionless upon the hulking shape of the image, wringing from it the knowledge of what its ugliness meant. And something in her throat swelled and swelled, and behind her eyelids burnt the sting of tears. Fiercely she fought back the weakness, desperately cast about for some way in which she might undo what she had unwittingly inflicted upon him.

And then all about her something intangible and grim began to form. Some iron presence that manifested itself only by the dark power she felt pressing upon her, stronger and stronger. Something coldly inimical to all things human. The black god's presence. The black god, come to defend his victim against one who was so alien to all his darkness—one who wept and trembled, and was warm with love and sorrow and desperate with despair.

She felt the inexorable force tightening around her, freezing her tears, turning the warmth and tenderness of her into gray ice, rooting her into a frigid immobility. The air dimmed about her, gray with cold, still with the utter deadness of the black god's unhuman presence. She had a glimpse of the dark place into which he was drawing her—a moveless, twilight place, deathlessly still. And an immense weight was pressing her down. The ice formed upon her soul, and the awful, iron despair which has no place among human emotions crept slowly through the fibers of her innermost self.

She felt herself turning into something cold and dark and rigid—a black image of herself—a black, hulking image to prison the spark of consciousness that still burned.

Then, as from a long way off in another time and world, came the memory of Guillaume's arms about her and the scornful press of his mouth over hers. It had not happened to her. It had happened to someone else, someone human and alive, in a far-away place. But the memory of it shot like fire through the rigidness of the body she had almost forgotten was hers, so cold and still it was—the memory of that curious, raging fever which was both hate and love. It broke the ice that bound her, for a moment only, and in that moment she fell to her knees at the dark statue's feet and burst into shuddering sobs, and the hot tears flowing were like fire to thaw her soul.

Slowly that thawing took place. Slowly the ice melted and the rigidity gave way, and the awful weight of the despair which was no human emotion lifted by degrees. The tears ran hotly between her fingers. But all about her she could feel, as tangibly as a touch, the imminence of the black god, waiting. And she knew her humanity, her weakness and transience, and the eternal, passionless waiting she could never hope to outlast. Her tears must run dry—and then—

She sobbed on, knowing herself in hopeless conflict with the vastness of death and oblivion, a tiny spark of warmth and life fighting vainly against the dark engulfing it; the perishable spark, struggling against inevitable extinction. For the black god was all death and nothingness, and the powers he drew upon were without limit—and all she had to fight him with was the flicker within her called life.

But suddenly in the depths of her despair she felt something stirring. A long, confused blurring passed over her, and another, and another, and the strangest emotions tumbled through her mind and vanished. Laughter and mirth, sorrow and tears and despair, love, envy, hate. She felt somehow a lessening in the oppressive peril about her, and she lifted her face from her hands.

Around the dark image a mist was swirling. It was tenuous and real by turns, but gradually she began to make out a ring of figures—girls' figures, more unreal than a vision—dancing girls who circled the crouching statue with flying feet and tossing hair—girls who turned to Jirel her own face in as many moods as there were girls. Jirel laughing, Jirel weeping, Jirel convulsed with fury, Jirel honey-sweet with love. Faster they swirled, a riot of flashing limbs, a chaos of tears and mirth and all humanity's moods. The air danced with them in shimmering waves, so that the land was blurred behind them and the image seemed to shiver within itself.

And she felt those waves of warmth and humanity beating insistently against the hovering chill which was the black god's presence. Life and warmth, fighting back the dark nothingness she had thought unconquerable. She felt it wavering about her as a canopy wavers in the wind. And slowly she felt it melting. Very gradually it lifted and dissipated, while the wild figures of gayety and grief and all kindred emotions whirled about the image and the beat of their aliveness pulsed through the air in heatwaves against the grayness of the god's cold.

And something in Jirel knew warmly that the image of life as a tiny spark flickering out in limitless black was a false one—that without light there can be no darkness—that death and life are interdependent, one upon the other. And that she, armored in the warmth of her aliveness, was the black god's equal, and a worthy

foe. It was an even struggle. She called up the forces of
life within her, feeling them hurled against the darkness, beating strongly upon the cold and silence of
oblivion. Strength flowed through her, and she knew
herself immortal in the power of life.

How long this went on she never knew. But she felt
victory pulsing like wine through her veins even before
the cold pall lifted. And it lifted quite suddenly. In a
breath, without warning, the black god's presence was
not. In that breath the swirling dancers vanished, and
the night was empty about her, and the singing of
triumph ran warmly through her body.

But the image—the image! The queerest change was
coming over it. The black, obscene outlines were unstable as mist. They quavered and shook, and ran together and somehow melted. . . .   The green moon
veiled its face again with clouds, and when the light
returned the image was no more than a black shadow
running fluidly upon the ground; a shadow which bore
the outlines of Guillaume—or what might have been
Guillaume. . . .

The moon-shadows moved across the livid disk, and
the shadow on the ground moved too, a monstrous
shadow latent with a terrible implication of the horrors
dormant within the being which cast the shadow, dreadful things that Guillaume might have been and done.
She knew then why the misshapen shadows were so
monstrous. They were a dim, leering hinting at what
might have been—what might yet be—frightful
suggestions of the dreadfulness dormant within every
living being. And the insane suggestions they made
were the more terrible because, impossible beyond

nightmares though they seemed, yet the mind intuitively recognized their truth. . . .

A little breeze sprang up fitfully, and the shadow moved, slipping over the stones without a sound. She found herself staggering after it on legs that shook, for the effort of that battle with the god had drained her of all strength. But the shadow was gliding faster now, and she dared not lose it. It floated on without a sound, now fast, now slow, its monstrous outlines shifting continually into patterns each more terribly significant than the last. She stumbled after it, the sword a dead weight in her hand, her red head hanging.

In five minutes she had lost all sense of direction. Beyond the hilltop the river ceased. The moving moonlight confused her and the stars traced queer pictures across the sky, from which she could get no bearings. The moon was overhead by now, and in those intervals when its clouds obscured the surface and the night was black around her, Guillaume's misshapen shadow vanished with the rest, and she suffered agonies of apprehension before the light came out again and she took up the chase anew.

The dark blot was moving now over a rolling meadowland dotted with queerly shaped trees. The grass over which she ran was velvet-soft, and she caught whiffs of perfume now and again from some tree that billowed with pale bloom in the moonlight. The shadow wavering ahead of her moved forward to pass one tall tree a little apart from the rest, its branches hanging in long, shaking streamers from its central crown. She saw the dark shape upon the ground pause as it neared the tree, and shiver a little, and then melt imperceptibly into the shadow cast by its branches.

That tree-shadow, until Guillaume's touched it, had borne the shape of a monster with crawling tentacles and flattened, thrusting head, but at the moment of conjunction the two melted into one—all the tentacles leaped forward to embrace the newcomer, and the two merged into an unnamably evil thing that lay upon the ground and heaved with a frightful aliveness of its own.

Jirel paused at its edge, looking down helplessly. She disliked to set her foot even upon the edge of that hideous black shape, though she knew intuitively that it could not harm her. The joined shadows were alive with menace and evil, but only to things in their own plane. She hesitated under the tree, wondering vainly how to part her lover's shade from the thing that gripped it. She felt somehow that his shadow had not joined the other altogether willingly. It was rather as if the evil instinct in the tree-shape had reached out to the evil in Guillaume, and by that evil held him, though the fineness that was still his revolted to the touch.

Then something brushed her shoulder gently, and lapped around her arm, and she leaped backward in a panic, too late. The tree's swinging branches had writhed round toward her, and one already was wrapped about her body. That shadow upon the ground had been a clear warning of the danger—a tentacled monster, lying in wait. Up swung her sword in a flash of green-tinged moonlight, and she felt the gripping branch yield like rubber under the blow. It gave amazingly and sprang back again, jerking her almost off her feet. She turned the blade against it, hewing desperately as she saw other branches curling around toward her. One had almost come within reach of her sword-arm, and was poising for the attack, when she felt her blade bite into the rubbery surface at last. Then with a root-deep shudder through all its members the tree loosed its hold and the severed limb fell writhing to the ground. Thick black sap dripped from the wound. And all the branches hung motionless, but upon the ground the shadow flung wildly agonized tentacles wide, and from the released grip Guillaume's shadow sprang free and glided away over the grass. Shaking with reaction, Jirel followed.

She gave more attention to the trees they passed now. There was one little shrub whose leaves blew constantly in shivering ripples, even when there was no wind, and its shadow was the shadow of a small leaping thing that hurled itself time and again against some invisible barrier and fell back, only to leap once more in panic terror. And one slim, leafless tree writhed against the stars with a slow, unceasing motion. It made no sound, but its branches twisted together and shuddered and strained in an agony more eloquent than speech. It seemed to wring its limbs together, agonized, dumb, with a slow anguish that never abated. And its shadow, dimly, was the shadow of a writhing woman.

And one tree, a miracle of bloom in the moonlight, swayed its ruffled branches seductively, sending out wave upon wave of intoxicating perfume and making a low, delightful humming, somehow like the melody of bees. Its shadow upon the ground was the shadow of a coiled serpent, lifting to strike.

Jirel was glad when they left the region of the trees and curved to the left down a long hill slope across which other shadows, without form, blew unceasingly with nothing to cast them. They raced noiselessly by, like wind-driven clouds. Among them she lost and found and lost again the shape she followed, until she grew dizzy from trying to keep her footing upon a ground that quavered with the blowing shadows so that she never knew upon what her feet were stepping, and the dim thing she followed was a nothingness that threaded its way in and out of the cloud-shapes bafflingly.

She had the idea now that the shadow of her lover was heading toward some definite goal. There was purpose in its dim gliding, and she looked ahead for some sign of the place it aimed toward. Below the hill the land stretched away featurelessly, cloud-mottled in the livid moonlight. Drifts of mist obscured it, and there were formless dark patches and pale blotches upon the night, and here and there a brook crawled across the blackness. She was completely lost now, for the river had long since vanished and she saw no hill which might have been the one upon which she had emerged.

They crossed another belt of quaking land, and the shadow gained upon her as she staggered over the jellylike surface. They came to a pale brook across which the shadow glided without a pause. It was a narrow, swift brook whose water chuckled thickly to itself in the dark. One stepping-stone broke the surface in the center of the stream, and she held her breath and leaped for it, not caring to slacken her pace. The stone gave under her foot like living flesh, and she thought she heard a groan, but she had gained the farther bank and did not pause to listen.

Then they were hurrying down another slope, the shadow gliding faster now, and more purposefully.

And the slope went down and down, steeply, until it became the side of a ravine and the rocks began to roll under her stumbling feet. She saw the fleeting shadow slip over a ledge and down a steep bank and then plunge into the darkness which lay like water along the bottom of the gully, and she gave a little sob of despair, for she knew now that she had lost it. But she struggled on into the dark that swallowed her up.

It was like wading deeper and deeper into a tangible oblivion. The blackness closed over her head, and she was groping through solid night. It filled the hollow in a thick flood, and in the depths of it she could even see the stars overhead. There was a moment of this blindness and groping, and then the moon rose.

Like a great leprous face it swung over the ravine's edge, the moon-clouds crawling across its surface. And that green light was an agony to her eyes, obscurely, achingly. It was like no mortal moonlight. It seemed endowed with a poisonous quality that was essentially a part of the radiance, and that unearthly, inexplicable light had an effect upon the liquid dark in the gully's bottom which no earthly moonlight could have had. It penetrated the blackness, broke it up into myriad struggling shadows that did not lie flat upon the ground, as all shadows should, but stood upright and three-dimensional and danced about her in a dizzy riot of nothingness taken shape. They brushed by her and through her without meeting obstruction, because for all their seeming solidity they were no more than shadows, without substance.

Among them danced the shape of Guillaume, and the outlines of it made her faint with terror, they were so like—and so dreadfully unlike—the Guillaume she had known, so leeringly suggestive of all the evil in him, and all the potential evil of mankind. The other shapes were ugly too, but they were the shapes of things whose real form she did not know, so that the implications latent in them she did not understand. But she missed no subtle half-tone of the full dreadfulness which was Guillaume, and her mind staggered with the suggestions the shadow-form made.

"Guillaume—" she heard herself sobbing, "Guillaume!" and realized that it was the first articulate sound which had passed her lips since she entered here. At her voice the reeling shadow slowed a little and hesitated, and then very reluctantly began to drift toward her through the spinning shades.

And then without warning something immeasurably cold and still closed down around her once more. The black god's presence. Again she felt herself congealing, through and through, as the ice of eternal nothingness thickened upon her soul and the gray, dim, formless place she remembered took shape about her and the immense weight of that iron despair descended again upon her shuddering spirit. If she had had warning she could have struggled, but it came so suddenly that before she could marshal her forces for the attack she was frigid to the core with the chill of unhumanity, and her body did not belong to her, and she was turning slowly into a black shadow that reeled among shadows in a dreadful, colorless void. . . .

Sharply through this stabbed the fire-hot memory that had wakened her before—the weight of a man's bearded mouth upon hers, the grip of his mailed arms.

And again she knew the flash of violence that might have been hate or love, and warmth flowed through her again in a sustaining tide.

And she fought. All the deeps of warmth and humanity in her she drew upon to fight the cold, all the violence of emotion to combat the terrible apathy which had gripped her once and was stretching out again for her soul.

It was not an easy victory. There were moments when the chill all but conquered, and moments when she felt herself drawn tenuously out of the congealing body which was hers to reel among the other shadows—a dim thing whose shape hinted at unspeakable possibilities, a shadow with form and depth and no reality. She caught remote beats of the insane harmony they danced to, and though her soul was fainting, her unreal shade went whirling on with the rest. She shared their torment for long minutes together.

But always she pulled herself free again. Always she fought back somehow into the ice-fettered body and shook off the frigid apathy that bound it, and hurled her weapons of life and vitality against the dark god's frosty presence.

And though she knew she would win this time, a little creeping doubt had entered her mind and would not be ousted. She could beat the god off, but she could never destroy him. He would always return. She dared not destroy him—a vision of her thought-picture came back to her, of the tiny life-spark burning against eternal darkness. And though if there were no light there could be no dark, yet it was true in reverse too, and if the power upon which the black god drew were destroyed—if the dark were dissipated, then there would be no light. No life. Interdependence, and eternal struggle. . . .

All this she was realizing with a remote part of herself as she fought. She realized it very vaguely, for her mind had not been trained to such abstractions. With her conscious self she was calling up the memories of love and hate and terror, the exultation of battle, the exaltation of joy. Everything that was alive and pulsing and warm she flung against the black god's chill, feeling her thoughts rise up in a protecting wall about her, to shut out all menace.

Victory, as before, came very suddenly. Without warning a blaze of light sprang up around her. The dark presence melted into oblivion. In that abrupt glare she closed her dazzled eyes, and when she opened them again familiar moonlight was flooding the glen. The fluid dark had vanished, the shadows no longer danced. That light had blasted them out of existence, and as it died she stared round the dim ravine with startled eyes, searching for the thing that was all she had seen of Guillaume. It was gone with the rest. The tangible dark which had brimmed the place was utterly gone. Not a shadow moved anywhere. But on the wind that was blowing down the ravine a small voice wailed.

And so again the weary chase went on. But she had less than ever to guide her now—only a fitful crying in the dark. "Jirel—" it wailed, "Jirel—Jirel—" and by that calling she followed. She could see nothing. Guillaume was no more than a voice now, and she could follow him by ear alone. Emptily the landscape stretched before her.

She had come out of the ravine's end upon a broad

fan-shaped slope which tilted downward into darkness. Water was falling somewhere near, but she could not see it. She ran blindly, ears strained for the small wailing cry. It led out over the slope and skirted the foot of a hill and passed by the place where water fell in a thin cascade down a cliffside, and whispered evilly to itself as it fell.

The sound obscured the sound she followed, and when she had passed beyond the whisper of the falls she had to stop and listen for a long time, while her heart thudded and the land around her crept with small, inexplicable noises, before she caught the far-away wail, "Jirel—Jirel—"

She set off in the direction from which the sound came, and presently heard it again more clearly, "Jirel! Jirel, my murderess!"

It was a heart-breaking course she ran, with no more than a fitful wailing to guide her and unknown perils lurking all about in the dark, and her own body and soul so drained of all strength by that second struggle with the god that the misty darkness wavered before her eyes and the ground underfoot heaved up to meet her time after time.

Once she fell, and lay still for a second to catch her struggling breath. But it seemed to her that the ground against her body was too warm, somehow, and moving gently as if with leisured breathing. So she leaped up again in swift alarm, and went skimming on with that dream-like speed over the dark grass.

It seemed to her that, as the shadow she had pursued had fled through shadowy places where she all but lost it time and again, now the fleeing voice led her through noisy places where she could scarcely hear it above the talking of brooks and the rush of falls and the blowing of the wind. She heard sounds she had never heard before—small, tenuous voices murmuring in the wind, the whispering of grass saying things in a murmurous language, the squeak of insects brushing past her face and somehow almost articulate. She had heard no birds here, though once a great, dark shapeless thing flapped heavily through the air a little distance ahead. But there were frog voices from the swamps she skirted, and hearing these she remembered what she had met in another swamp on her first visit here, and a little chill went down her back.

In every sound she heard ran the thread of evil inextricably tangled with a thread of purest despair—a human despair even through the grasses' rustling and in the murmur of the wind—voices wailing so hopelessly that more than once tears started unbidden to her eyes, but so indistinctly that she could never be sure she had heard. And always through the wailing rippled the chuckle of dim evils without any names in human languages. And with all these sounds she heard many others that meant nothing to her and upon whose origins she dared not speculate.

Through this welter of incomprehensible noises she followed the one far crying that had meaning for her. It led in a long arc across rolling ground, over muttering brooks that talked morbidly in the dark. Presently she began to catch faint strains of the most curious music. It did not have the quality of composition, or even unity, but seemed to consist of single groups of notes, like sprays of music, each unrelated to the rest, as if thousands of invisible creatures were piping tiny, primitive tunes, every one deaf to the songs of his fellows. The sound grew louder as she advanced, and she saw that she was coming to a luminous patch upon the dark ground. When she reached the edge she paused in wonder.

The music was rising from the earth, and it rose visibly. She could actually see the separate strains wavering upward through the still air. She could never have described what she saw, for the look of that visible music was beyond any human words. Palely the notes rose, each singing its tiny, simple tune. There seemed to be no discords, for all the non-unity of the sounds. She had the mad fancy that the music was growing— that if she wished she could wade through the ranks of it and gather great sheaves of sound—perhaps bouquets which, if they were carefully selected, would join together and play a single complex melody.

But it was not music she dared listen to long. There was in it the queerest little gibbering noise, and as she lingered that sound intensified and ran through her brain in small, giggling undernotes, and she caught herself laughing senselessly at nothing at all. Then she took fright, and listened for the voice that was Guillaume. And terrifyingly she heard it strongly in the very midst of the little mad jinglings. It deepened and grew, and drowned out the smaller sounds, and the whole field was one vast roar of insane laughter that thundered through her head in destroying waves—a jarring laughter that threatened to shake her body irresistibly and wrung tears from her eyes even as she laughed.

"Guillaume!" she called again in the midst of her agony. "Oh Guillaume!" and at the sound of her voice all laughter ceased and a vast, breathless silence fell upon the whole dark world. Through that silence the tiniest wail threaded itself reedily, "Jirel—" Then other sounds came back to life, and the wind blew and the wail diminished in the distance. Again the chase went on.

By now the moon's dead, crawling face had sunk nearly to the horizon, and the shadows lay in long patterns across the ground. It seemed to her that around the broad ring of the sky a pallor was rising. In her weariness and despair she did not greatly care now, knowing though she did that should day catch her here it meant a death more terrible than any man can die on earth, and an eternity, perhaps, of torment in one of the many shapes she had seen and recognized as the spirits of the damned. Perhaps a writhing tree—or imprisonment in an obscenely reveltory image, like Guillaume—or no more than a wailing along the wind for ever. She was too tired to care. She stumbled on hopelessly, hearing the voice that cried her name grow fainter and fainter in the distance.

The end of the chase came very suddenly. She reached a stream that flowed smoothly under the arch of a low, dark bridge, and crossed over it, seeing her face look up at her from the water with a wild mouthing of soundless cries, though her own lips were closed. She met her reflected eyes and read warning and despair and the acutest agony in their depths, and saw her own face writhing all out of familiarity with anguish and hopelessness. It was a frightful vision, but she scarcely saw it, and ran on without heeding the image in the water or the landscape around her or even the broadening dawn around the horizon.

Then close ahead of her sounded the thin small voice

she followed, and she woke out of her stupor and stared around. That bridge had not ended upon the far side of the brook, but somehow had arched up its sides and broadened its floor and become a dark temple around whose walls ran a more bestial sculpture than anything imagined even in dreams. Here in this carved and columned building was the epitome of the whole dim hell through which she had been running. Here in these sculptures she read all the hideous things the shadows had hinted at, all the human sorrow and despair and hopelessness she had heard in the wind's crying, all the chuckling evil that the water spoke. In the carvings she could trace the prisoned souls of men and beasts, tormented in many ways, some of which she had already seen, but many that she had not, and which she mercifully could not understand. It was not clear for what they were punished, save that the torture was tinged just enough with justice so that it seemed the more hideously unjust in its exaggerations. She closed her eyes and stood swaying a little, feeling the triumphant evil of the temple pulsing around her, too stunned and sick even to wonder what might come next.

Then the small voice was beating around her head. Almost she felt the desperate hammering of wings, as if some little, frantic bird were flying against her face. "Jirel!—Jirel!" it cried in the purest agony, over and over, a final, wild appeal. And she did not know what to do. Helplessly she stood there, feeling it beating round her head, feeling the temple's obscene triumph surging through her.

And without warning, for the third time the black god's presence folded like a cloak about her. Almost she welcomed it. Here was something she knew how to fight. As from a long distance away she heard the small voice crying in diminishing echoes, and the frigid twilight was forming about her, and the gray ice thickened upon her soul. She called up the memories of hate and love and anger to hurl against it, thinking as she did so that perhaps one who had lived less violently than herself and had lesser stores of passions to recall might never be able to combat the god's death-chill. She remembered laughter, and singing and gayety— she remembered slaughter and blood and the wild clang of mail—she remembered kisses in the dark, and the hard grip of men's arms about her body.

But she was weary, and the dawn was breaking terribly along the sky, and the dark god's power was rooted in a changeless oblivion that never faltered. And she began to realize failure. The memories she flung out had no power against the gray pall of that twilight place wherein he dwelt, and she knew the first seeping of the iron despair through her brain. Gradually the will to struggle congealed with her congealing body, until she was no longer a warm, vital thing of flesh and blood, but something rigid and ice-bound, dwelling bodilessly in the twilight.

There was one small spark of her that the god could not freeze. She felt him assailing it. She felt him driving it out of the cold thing that had been her body—drawing it forth irresistibly—she was a thin, small crying in the dark. . . . Helplessly she felt herself whirling to and fro upon currents she had never felt before, and dashing against unseen obstacles, wailing wordlessly. She had no substance, and the world had faded from around her. She was aware of other things—dim, vague, like beating pulses, that were whirling through the dark, small lost things like herself, bodiless and unprotected, buffeted by every current that blew; little wailing things, shrieking through the night.

Then one of the small vaguenesses blew against her and through her, and in the instant of its passage she caught the faint vibration of her name, and knew that this was the voice that had summoned her out of her dreams, the voice she had pursued: Guillaume. And with that instant's union something as sustaining as life itself flashed through her wonderfully, a bright spark that swelled and grew and blazed, and—

She was back again in her body amidst the bestial carvings of the temple—a thawing, warming body from which the shackles of icy silence were falling, and that hot blaze was swelling still, until all of her being was suffused and pulsing with it, and the frigid pall of dark melted away unresistingly before the hot, triumphant blaze that dwelt within her.

In her ecstasy of overwhelming warmth she scarcely realized her victory. She did not greatly care. Something very splendid was happening. . . .

Then the air trembled, and all about her small, thin sounds went shivering upward, as if ribbons of high screams were rippling past her across a background of silence. The blaze within her faded slowly, paled, imperceptibly died away, and the peace of utter emptiness flooded into her soul. She turned wearily backward across the bridge. Behind her the temple stood in a death-like quiet. The evil that had beat in long pulses through it was stilled for a while by something stunningly splendid which had no place in the starry hell; something human and alive, something compounded of love and longing, near-despair and sacrifice and triumph.

Jirel did not realize how great a silence she left behind, nor very clearly what she had done. Above her against the paling sky she saw a familiar hilltop, and dimly knew that in all her long night of running she had been circling round toward her starting-place. She was too numb to care. She was beyond relief or surprise.

She began the climb passionlessly, with no triumph in the victory she knew was hers at last. For she had driven Guillaume out of the image and into the shadow, and out of the shadow into the voice, and out of the voice into—clean death, perhaps. She did not know. But he had found peace, for his insistences no longer beat upon her consciousness. And she was content.

Above her the cave mouth yawned. She toiled up the slope, dragging her sword listlessly, weary to the very soul, but quite calm now, with a peace beyond all understanding.

Jirel Meets Magic

Over Guischard's fallen drawbridge thundered Joiry's warrior lady, sword swinging, voice shouting hoarsely inside her helmet. The scarlet plume of her crest rippled in the wind. Straight into the massed defenders at the gate she plunged, careering through them by the very impetuosity of the charge, the weight of her mighty warhorse opening up a gap for the men at her heels to widen. For a while there was tumult unspeakable there under the archway, the yells of fighters and the clang of mail on mail and the screams of stricken men. Jirel of Joiry was a shouting battle-machine from which Guischard's men reeled in bloody confusion as she whirled and slashed and slew in the narrow confines of the gateway, her great stallion's iron hoofs weapons as potent as her own whistling blade.

In her full armor she was impregnable to the men on foot, and the horse's armor protected him from their vengeful blades, so that alone, almost, she might have won the gateway. By sheer weight and impetuosity she carried the battle through the defenders under the arch. They gave way before the mighty war-horse and his screaming rider. Jirel's swinging sword and the stallion's trampling feet cleared a path for Joiry's men to follow, and at last into Guischard's court poured the steel-clad hordes of Guischard's conquerors.

Jirel's eyes were yellow with blood-lust behind the helmet bars, and her voice echoed savagely from the steel cage that confined it. "Giraud! Bring me Giraud! A gold piece to the man who brings me the wizard Giraud!"

She waited impatiently in the courtyard, reining her excited charger in mincing circles over the flags, unable to dismount alone in her heavy armor and disdainful of the threats of possible arbalesters in the arrow-slits that looked down upon her from Guischard's frowning gray walls. A crossbow shaft was the only thing she had to fear in her impregnable mail.

She waited in mounting impatience, a formidable figure in her bloody armor, the great sword lying across her saddlebow and her eager, angry voice echoing hoarsely from the helmet, "Giraud! Make haste, you varlets! Bring me Giraud!"

There was such bloodthirsty impatience in that hollowly booming voice that the men who were returning from searching the castle hung back as they crossed the court toward their lady in reluctant twos and threes, failure eloquent upon their faces.

"What!" screamed Jirel furiously. "You, Giles! Have you brought me Giraud? Watkin! Where is that wizard Giraud? Answer me, I say!"

"We've scoured the castle, my lady," said one of

the men fearfully as the angry voice paused. "The wizard is gone."

"Now God defend me!" groaned Joiry's lady. "God help a poor woman served by fools! Did you search among the slain?"

"We searched everywhere, Lady Jirel. Giraud has escaped us."

Jirel called again upon her Maker in a voice that was blasphemy itself.

"Help me down, then, you hell-spawned knaves," she grated. "I'll find him myself. He must be here!"

With difficulty they got her off the sidling horse. It took two men to handle her, and a third to steady the charger. All the while they struggled with straps and buckles she cursed them hollowly, emerging limb by limb from the casing of steel and swearing with a soldier's fluency as the armor came away. Presently she stood free on the bloody flagstones, a slim, straight lady, keen as a blade, her red hair a flame to match the flame of her yellow eyes. Under the armor she wore a tunic of link-mail from the Holy Land, supple as silk and almost as light, and a doeskin shirt to protect the milky whiteness of her skin.

She was a creature of the wildest paradox, this warrior lady of Joiry, hot as a red coal, chill as steel, satiny of body and iron of soul. The set of her chin was firm, but her mouth betrayed a tenderness she would have died before admitting. But she was raging now.

"Follow me, then, fools!" she shouted. "I'll find that God-cursed wizard and split his head with this sword if it takes me until the day I die. I swear it. I'll teach him what it costs to ambush Joiry men. By heaven, he'll pay with his life for my ten who fell at

Massy Ford last week. The foul spell-brewer! He'll learn what it means to defy Joiry!''

Breathing threats and curses, she strode across the court, her men following reluctantly at her heels and casting nervous glances upward at the gray towers of Guischard. It had always borne a bad name this ominous castle of the wizard Giraud, a place where queer things happened, which no man entered uninvited and whence no prisoner had ever escaped, though the screams of torture echoed often from its walls. Jirel's men would have followed her straight through the gates of hell, but they stormed Guischard at her heels with terror in their hearts and no hope of conquest.

She alone seemed not to know fear of the dark sorcerer. Perhaps it was because she had known things so dreadful that mortal perils held no terror for her—there were whispers at Joiry of their lady, and of things that had happened there which no man dared think on. But when Guischard fell, and the wizard's defenders fled before Jirel's mightly steed and the onrush of Joiry's men, they had plucked up heart, thinking that perhaps the ominous tales of Giraud had been gossip only, since the castle fell as any ordinary lord's castle might fall. But now—there were whispers again, and nervous glances over the shoulder, and men huddled together as they re-entered Guischard at their lady's hurrying heels. A castle from which a wizard might vanish into thin air, with all the exits watched, must be a haunted place, better burned and forgotten. They followed Jirel reluctantly, half ashamed but fearful.

In Jirel's stormy heart there was no room for terror as she plunged into the gloom of the archway that opened upon Guischard's great central hall. Anger that the man might have escaped her was a torch to light the way, and she paused in that door with eager anticipation, sweeping the corpse-strewn hall at a glance, searching for some clue to explain how her quarry had disappeared.

"He can't have escaped," she told herself confidently. "There's no way out. He *must* be here somewhere." And she stepped into the hall, turning over the bodies she passed with a careless foot to make sure that death had not robbed her of vengeance.

An hour later, as they searched the last tower, she was still telling herself that the wizard could not have gone without her knowledge. She had taken special pains about that. There was a secret passage to the river, but she had had that watched. And an underwater door opened into the moat, but he could not have gone that way without meeting her men. Secret paths lay open; she had found them all and posted a guard at each, and Giraud had not left the castle by any door that led out. She climbed the stairs of the last tower wearily, her confidence shaken.

An iron-barred oaken door closed the top of the steps, and Jirel drew back as her men lifted the heavy crosspieces and opened it for her. It had not been barred from within. She stepped into the little round room inside, hope fading completely as she saw that it too was empty, save for the body of a page-boy lying on the uncarpeted floor. Blood had made a congealing pool about him, and as Jirel looked she saw something which roused her flagging hopes. Feet had trodden in that blood, not the mailed feet of armed men, but the tread of shapeless cloth shoes such as surely none but Giraud would have worn when the castle was besieged and falling, and every man's help needed. Those bloody tracks led straight across the room toward the wall, and in that wall—a window.

Jirel stared. To her a window was a narrow slit deep in stone, made for the shooting of arrows, and never covered save in the coldest weather. But this window was broad and low, and instead of the usual animal pelt for hangings a curtain of purple velvet had been drawn back to disclose shutters carved out of something that might have been ivory had any beast alive been huge enough to yield such great unbroken sheets of whiteness. The shutters were unlatched, swinging slightly ajar, and upon them Jirel saw the smear of bloody fingers.

With a little triumphant cry she sprang forward. Here, then, was the secret way Giraud had gone. What lay beyond the window she could not guess. Perhaps an unsuspected passage, or a hidden room. Laughing exultantly, she swung open the ivory shutters.

There was a gasp from the men behind her. She did not hear it. She stood quite still, staring with incredulous eyes. For those ivory gates had opened upon no dark stone hiding-place or secret tunnel. They did not reveal the afternoon sky outside, nor did they admit the shouts of her men still subduing the last of the defenders in the court below. Instead she was looking out upon a green woodland over which brooded a violet day like no day she had ever seen before. In paralyzed amazement she looked down, seeing not the bloody flags of the courtyard far below, but a mossy carpet at a level with the floor. And on that moss she saw the mark of blood-stained feet. This window might be a magic one, opening into strange lands, but through it had gone the man she swore to kill, and where he fled she must follow.

She lifted her eyes from the tracked moss and stared out again through the dimness under the trees. It was a lovelier land than anything seen even in dreams; so lovely that it made her heart ache with its strange, unearthly enchantment—green woodland hushed and brooding in the hushed violet day. There was a promise of peace there, and forgetfulness and rest. Suddenly the harsh, shouting, noisy world behind her seemed very far away and chill. She moved forward and laid her hand upon the ivory shutters, staring out.

The shuffle of scared men behind her awakened Jirel from the enchantment that had gripped her. She turned. The dreamy magic of the woodland loosed its hold as she faced the men again, but its memory lingered. She shook her red head a little, meeting their fearful eyes. She nodded toward the open window.

"Giraud has gone out there," she said. "Give me your dagger, Giles. This sword is too heavy to carry far."

"But lady—Lady Jirel—dear lady—you can't— can't go out there—Saint Guilda save us! Lady Jirel!"

Jirel's crisp voice cut short the babble of protest.

"Your dagger, Giles. I've sworn to slay Giraud, and slay him I shall, in whatever land he hides. Giles!"

A man-at-arms shuffled forward with averted face, handing her his dagger. She gave him the sword she carried and thrust the long-bladed knife into her belt. She turned again to the window. Green and cool and lovely, the woodland lay waiting. She thought as she set her knee upon the sill that she must have explored this violet calm even had her oath not driven her; for there was an enchantment about the place that drew her irresistibly. She pulled up her other knee and jumped lightly. The mossy ground received her without a jar.

For a few moments Jirel stood very still, watching, listening. Bird songs trilled intermittently about her, and breezes stirred the leaves. From very far away she thought she caught the echoes of a song when the wind blew, and there was something subtly irritating about its simple melody that seemed to seesaw endlessly up and down on two notes. She was glad when the wind died and the song no longer shrilled in her ears.

It occurred to her that before she ventured far she must mark the window she had entered by, and she turned curiously, wondering how it looked from this side. What she saw sent an inexplicable little chill down her back. Behind her lay a heap of moldering ruins, moss-grown, crumbling into decay. Fire had blackened the stones in ages past. She could see that it must have been a castle, for the original lines of it were not yet quite lost. Only one low wall remained standing now, and in it opened the window through which she had come. There was something hauntingly familiar about the lines of those moldering stones, and she turned away with a vague unease, not quite understanding why. A little path wound away under the low-hanging trees, and she followed it slowly, eyes alert for signs that Giraud had passed this way. Birds trilled drowsily in the leaves overhead, queer, unrecognizable songs like the music of no birds she knew. The violet light was calm and sweet about her.

She had gone on in the bird-haunted quiet for many

minutes before she caught the first hint of anything at odds with the perfect peace about her. A whiff of wood-smoke drifted to her nostrils on a vagrant breeze. When she rounded the next bend of the path she saw what had caused it. A tree lay across the way in a smother of shaking leaves and branches. She knew that she must skirt it, for the branches were too tangled to penetrate, and she turned out of the path, following the trunk toward its broken base.

She had gone only a few steps before the sound of a curious sobbing came to her ears. It was the gasp of choked breathing, and she had heard sounds like that too often before not to know that she approached death in some form or another. She laid her hand on her knife-hilt and crept forward softly.

The tree trunk had been severed as if by a blast of heat, for the stump was charred black and still smoking. Beyond the stump a queer tableau was being enacted, and she stopped quite still, staring through the leaves.

Upon the moss a naked girl was lying, gasping her life out behind the hands in which her face was buried. There was no mistaking the death-sound in that failing breath, although her body was unmarked. Hair of a strange green-gold pallor streamed over her bare white body, and by the fragility and tenuosity of that body Jirel knew that she could not be wholly human.

Above the dying girl a tall woman stood. And that woman was a magnet for Jirel's fascinated eyes. She was generously curved, sleepy-eyed. Black hair bound her head sleekly, and her skin was like rich, dark, creamy velvet. A violet robe wrapped her carelessly, leaving arms and one curved shoulder bare, and her girdle was a snake of something like purple glass. It might have been carved from some vast jewel, save for its size and unbroken clarity. Her feet were thrust bare into silver sandals. But it was her face that held Jirel's yellow gaze.

The sleepy eyes under heavily drooping lids were purple as gems, and the darkly crimson mouth curled in a smile so hateful that fury rushed up in Jirel's heart as she watched. That lazy purple gaze dwelt aloofly upon the gasping girl on the moss. The woman was saying in a voice as rich and deep as thick-piled velvet:

"—nor will any other of the dryad folk presume to work forbidden magic in my woodlands for a long, long while to come. Your fate shall be a deadly example to them, Irsla. You dared too greatly. None who defy Jarisme live. Hear me, Irsla!"

The sobbing breath had slowed as the woman spoke, as if life were slipping fast from the dryad-girl on the moss; and as she realized it the speaker's arm lifted and a finger of white fire leaped from her outstretched hand, stabbing the white body at her feet. And the girl Irsla started like one shocked back into life.

"Hear me out, dryad! Let your end be a warning to—"

The girl's quickened breath slowed again as the white brilliance left her, and again the woman's hand rose, again the light-blade stabbed. From behind her shielding hands the dryad gasped:

"Oh, mercy, mercy, Jarisme! Let me die!"

"When I have finished. Not before. Life and death are mine to command here, and I am not yet done with you. Your stolen magic—"

She paused, for Irsla had slumped once more upon the moss, breath scarcely stirring her. As Jarisme's light-dealing hand rose for the third time Jirel leapt forward. Partly it was intuitive hatred of the lazy-eyed woman, partly revolt at this cat-and-mouse play with a dying girl for a victim. She swung her arm in an arc that cleared the branches from her path, and called out in her clear, strong voice:

"Have done, woman! Let her die in peace."

Slowly Jarisme's purple eyes rose. They met Jirel's hot yellow glare. Almost physical impact was in that first meeting of their eyes, and hatred flashed between them instantly, like the flash of blades—the instinctive hatred of total opposites, born enemies. Each stiffened subtly, as cats do in the instant before combat. But Jirel thought she saw in the purple gaze, behind all its kindling anger, a faint disquiet, a nameless uncertainty.

"Who are you?" asked Jarisme, very softly, very dangerously.

Something in that unsureness behind her angry eyes prompted Jirel to answer boldly:

"Jirel of Joiry. I seek the wizard Giraud, who fled me here. Stop tormenting that wretched girl and tell me where to find him. I can make it worth your while."

Her tone was imperiously mandatory, and behind Jarisme's drooping lips an answering flare of anger lighted, almost drowning out that faint unease.

"You do not know me," she observed, her voice very gentle. "I am the sorceress Jarisme, and high ruler over all this land. Did you think to buy me, then, earth-woman?"

Jirel smiled her sweetest, most poisonous smile.

"You will forgive me," she purred. "At the first glance at you I did not think your price could be high. . ."

A petty malice had inspired the speech, and Jirel was sorry as it left her lips, for she knew that the scorn which blazed up in Jarisme's eyes was justified. The sorceress made a contemptuous gesture of dismissal.

"I shall waste no more of my time here," she said. "Get back to your little lands, Jirel of Joiry, and tempt me no further."

The purple gaze rested briefly on the motionless dryad at her feet, flicked Jirel's hot eyes with a glance of scorn which yet did not wholly hide that curious uncertainty in its depths. One hand slid behind her, oddly as if she were seeking a door-latch in empty air. Then like a heat-shimmer the air danced about her, and in an instant she was gone.

Jirel blinked. Her ears had deceived her as well as her eyes, she thought, for as the sorceress vanished a door closed softly somewhere. Yet look though she would, the green glade was empty, the violet air untroubled. No Jarisme anywhere—no door. Jirel shrugged after a moment's bewilderment. She had met magic before.

A sound from the scarcely breathing girl upon the moss distracted her, and she dropped to her knees beside the dying dryad. There was no mark or wound upon her, yet Jirel knew that death could be only a matter of moments. And dimly she recalled that, so legend said, a tree-sprite never survived the death of its tree. Gently she turned the girl over, wondering if she were beyond help.

At the feel of those gentle hands the dryad's lips quivered and rose. Brook-brown eyes looked up at Jirel, with green swimming in their deeps like leaf-reflection in a woodland pool.

"My thanks to you," faltered the girl in a ghostly murmur. "But get you back to your home now—before Jarisme's anger slays you."

Jirel shook her red head stubbornly.

"I must find Giraud first, and kill him, as I have sworn to do. But I will wait. Is there anything I can do?"

The green-reflecting eyes searched hers for a moment. The dryad must have read resolution there, for she shook her head a little.

"I must die—with my tree. But if you are determined—hear me. I owe you—a debt. There is a talisman—braided in my hair. When I—am dead—take it. It is Jarisme's sign. All her subjects wear them. It will guide you to her—and to Giraud. He is ever beside her. I know. I think it was her anger at you—that made her forget to take it from me, after she had dealt me my death. But why she did not slay you—I do not know. Jarisme is quick—to kill. No matter—listen now. If you must have Giraud—you must take a risk that no one here—has ever taken—before. Break this talisman—at Jarisme's feet. I do not know—what will happen then. Something—very terrible. It releases powers—even she can not control. It may—destroy you too. But—it is—a chance. May you—have—all good—"

The faltering voice failed. Jirel, bending her head, caught only meaningless murmurs that trailed away to nothing. The green-gold head dropped suddenly forward on her sustaining arm. Through the forest all about her went one long, quivering sigh, as if an intangible breeze ruffled the trees. Yet no leaves stirred.

Jirel bent and kissed the dryad's forehead, then laid

her very gently back on the moss. And as she did so her hand in the masses of strangely colored hair came upon something sharp and hard. She remembered the talisman. It tingled in her fingers as she drew it out—an odd little jagged crystal sparkling with curious aliveness from the fire burning in its heart.

When she had risen to her feet, leaving the dead dryad lying upon the moss which seemed so perfectly her couch, she saw that the inner brilliance streaming in its wedge-shaped pattern through the crystal was pointing a quivering apex forward and to the right. Irsla had said it would guide her. Experimentally she twisted her hand to the left. Yes, the shaking light shifted within the crystal, pointing always toward the right, and Jarisme.

One last long glance she gave to the dryad on the moss. Then she set off again down the path, the little magical thing stinging her hand as she walked. And as she went she wondered. This strong hatred which had flared so instinctively between her and the sorceress was not enough to burn any trace of fear from her mind, and she remembered that look of uncertainty in the purple gaze that had shot such hatred at her. Why? Why had she not been slain as Irsla was slain, for defiance of this queer land's ruler?

For a while she paced unheedingly along under the trees. Then abruptly the foliage ceased and a broad meadow lay before her, green in the clear, violet day. Beyond the meadow the slim shaft of a tower rose dazzlingly white, and toward it in steady radiance that magical talisman pointed.

From very far away she thought she still caught the echoes of that song when the wind blew, an irritating monotony that made her ears ache. She was glad when the wind died and the song no longer shrilled in her ears.

Out across the meadow she went. Far ahead she could make out purple mountains like low clouds on the horizon, and here and there in the distances clumps of woodland dotted the meadows. She walked on more rapidly now, for she was sure that the white tower housed Jarisme, and with her Giraud. And she must have gone more swiftly than she knew, for with almost magical speed the shining shaft drew nearer.

She could see the arch of its doorway, bluely violet within. The top of the shaft was battlemented, and she caught splashes of color between the teeth of the stone scarps, as if flowers were massed there and spilling blossoms against the whiteness of the tower. The singsong music was louder than ever, and much nearer. Jirel's heart beat a bit heavily as she advanced, wondering what sort of a sorceress this Jarisme might be, what dangers lay before her in the path of her vow's fulfillment. Now the white tower rose up over her, and she was crossing the little space before the door, peering in dubiously. All she could see was dimness and violet mist.

She laid her hand upon the dagger, took a deep breath and stepped boldly in under the arch. In the instant her feet left the solid earth she saw that this violet mist filled the whole shaft of the tower, that there was no floor. Emptiness engulfed her, and all reality ceased.

She was falling through clouds of violet blackness, but in no recognizable direction. It might have been up, down, or sidewise through space. Everything had vanished in the violet nothing. She knew an endless moment of vertigo and rushing motion; then the dizzy emptiness vanished in a breath and she was standing in a gasping surprise upon the roof of Jarisme's tower.

She knew where she was by the white battlements ringing her round, banked with strange blossoms in muted colors. In the center of the circular, marble-paved place a low couch, cushioned in glowing yellow, stood in the midst of a heap of furs. Two people sat side by side on the couch. One was Giraud. Black-robed, dark-visaged, he stared at Jirel with a flicker of disquiet in his small, dull eyes. He said nothing.

Jirel dismissed him with a glance, scarcely realizing his presence. For Jarisme had lowered from her lips a long, silver flute. Jirel realized that the queer, maddening music must have come from that gleaming length, for it no longer echoed in her ears. Jarisme was holding the instrument now in midair, regarding Jirel over it with a purple-eyed gaze that was somehow thoughtful and a little apprehensive, though anger glowed in it, too.

"So," she said richly, in her slow, deep voice. "For the second time you defy me."

At these words Giraud turned his head sharply and stared at the sorceress' impassive profile. She did not return his gaze, but after a moment he looked quickly back at Jirel, and in his eyes too she saw that flicker of alarm, and with it a sort of scared respect. It puzzled her, and she did not like being puzzled. She said a little breathlessly:

"If you like, yes. Give me that skulking potion-brewer beside you and set me down again outside this damned tower of trickery. I came to kill your pet spellmonger here for treachery done me in my own world by this creature who dared not stay to face me.''

Her peremptory words hung in the air like the echoes of a gong. For a while no one spoke. Jarisme smiled more subtly than before, an insolent, slow smile that made Jirel's pulses hammer with the desire to smash it down the woman's lush, creamy throat. At last Jarisme said, in a voice as rich and deep as thick-piled velvet:

"Hot words, hot words, soldier-woman! Do you really imagine that your earthly squabbles matter to Jarisme?''

"What matters to Jarisme is of little moment to me,'' Jirel said contemptuously. "All I want is this skulker here, whom I have sworn to kill.''

Jarisme's slow smile was maddening. "You demand it of me—Jarisme?'' She asked with soft incredulity. "Only fools offend me, woman, and they but once. None commands me. You will have to learn that.''

Jirel smiled thinly. "At what price, then, do you value your pet cur?''

Giraud half rose from the couch at that last insult, his dark face darker with a surge of anger. Jarisme pushed him back with a lazy hand.

"This is between your—friend—and me,'' she said. "I do not think, soldier''—the appellation was the deadliest of insults in the tone she used—''that any price you could offer would interest me.''

"And yet your interest is very easily caught.'' Jirel flashed a contemptuous glance at Giraud, restive under the woman's restraining hand.

Jarisme's rich pallor flushed a little. Her voice was sharper as she said:

"Do not tempt me too far, earthling."

Jirel's yellow eyes defied her. "I am not afraid."

The sorceress' purple gaze surveyed her slowly. When Jarisme spoke again a tinge of reluctant admiration lightened the slow scorn of her voice.

"No—you are not afraid. And a fool not to be. Fools annoy me, Jirel of Joiry."

She laid the flute down on her knee and lazily lifted a ringless hand. Anger was glowing in her eyes now, blotting out all trace of that little haunting fear. But Giraud caught the rising hand, bending, whispering urgently in her ear. Jirel caught a part of what he said: "—what happens to those who tamper with their own destiny—" And she saw the anger fade from the sorceress' face as apprehension brightened there again. Jarisme looked at Jirel with a long, hard look and shrugged her ample shoulders.

"Yes," she murmured. "Yes, Giraud. It is wisest so." And to Jirel, "Live then, earthling. Find your way back to your own land if you can, but I warn you, do not trouble me again. I shall not stay my hand if our paths ever cross in the future."

She struck her soft, white palms together sharply. And at the sound the roof-top and the violet sky and the banked flowers at the parapets whirled around Jirel in dizzy confusion. From very far away she heard that clap of peremptory hands still echoing, but it seemed to her that the great, smokily colored blossoms were undergoing an inexplicable transformation. They quivered and spread and thrust upward from the edges of the tower to arch over her head. Her feet were pressing a mossy ground, and the sweet, earthy odors of a garden rose about her. Blinking, she stared around as the world slowly steadied.

She was no longer on the roof-top. As far as she could see through the tangled stems, great flowering plants sprang up in the gloaming of a strange, enchanted forest. She was completely submerged in greenery, and the illusion of under-water filled her eyes, for the violet light that filtered through the leaves was diffused and broken into a submarine dimness. Uncertainly she began to grope her way forward, staring about to see what sort of a miracle had enfolded her.

It was a bower in fairyland. She had come into a tropical garden of great, muted blooms and jungle silences. In the diffused light the flowers nodded sleepily among the leaves, hypnotically lovely, hypnotically soporific with their soft colors and drowsy, never-ending motion. The fragrance was overpowering. She went on slowly, treading moss that gave back no sound. Here under the canopy of leaves was a little separate world of color and silence and perfume. Dreamily she made her way among the flowers.

Their fragrance was so strongly sweet that it went to her head, and she walked in a waking dream. Because of this curious, scented trance in which she went she was never quite sure if she had actually seen that motion among the leaves, and looked closer, and made out a huge, incredible serpent of violet transparency, a giant replica of the snake that girdled Jarisme's waist, but miraculously alive, miraculously supple and gliding, miraculously twisting its soundless way among the blossoms and staring at her with impassive, purple eyes.

While it glided along beside her she had other strange visions too, and could never remember just what they were, or why she caught familiar traces in the tiny, laughing faces that peered at her from among the flowers, or half believed the wild, impossible things they whispered to her, their laughing mouths brushing her ears as they leaned down among the blossoms.

The branches began to thin at last, as she neared the edge of the enchanted place. She walked slowly, half conscious of the great transparent snake like a living jewel writhing along soundlessly at her side, her mind vaguely troubled in its dream by the fading remembrance of what those little, merry voices had told her. When she came to the very edge of the bowery jungle and broke out into clear daylight again she stopped in a daze, staring round in the brightening light as the perfumes slowly cleared from her head.

Sanity and realization returned to her at last. She shook her red head dizzily and looked round, half expecting, despite her returning clarity, to see the great serpent gliding across the grass. But there was nothing. Of course she had dreamed. Of course those little laughing voices had not told her that—that—she clutched after the vanishing tags of remembrance, and caught nothing. Ruefully she laughed and brushed away the clinging memories, looking round to see where she was.

She stood at the crest of a little hill. Below her the flower-fragrant jungle nodded, a little patch of enchanted greenery clothing the slopes of the hill. Beyond and below green meadows stretched away to a far-off line of forest which she thought she recognized as that in which she had first met Jarisme. But the white tower which had risen in the midst of the meadows was magically gone. Where it had stood, unbroken greenery lay under the violet clarity of the sky.

As she stared round in bewilderment a faint prickling stung her palm, and she glanced down, remembering the talisman clutched in her hand. The quivering light was streaming in a long wedge toward some point behind her. She turned. She was in the foothills of those purple mountains she had glimpsed from the edge of the woods. High and shimmering, they rose above her. And, hazily in the heat-waves that danced among their heights, she saw the tower.

Jirel groaned to herself. Those peaks were steep and rocky. Well, no help for it. She must climb. She growled a soldier's oath in her throat and turned wearily toward the rising slopes. They were rough and deeply slashed with ravines. Violet heat beat up from the reflecting rocks, and tiny, brilliantly colored things scuttled from her path—orange lizards and coral red scorpions and little snakes like bright blue jewels.

It seemed to her as she stumbled upward among the broken stones that the tower was climbing too. Time after time she gained upon it, and time after time when she lifted her eyes after a grueling struggle up steep ravines, that mocking flicker of whiteness shimmered still high and unattainable on some distant peak. It had the mistiness of unreality, and if her talisman's guide had not pointed steadily upward she would have thought it an illusion to lead her astray.

But after what seemed hours of struggle, there came the time when, glancing up, she saw the shaft rising on

the topmost peak of all, white as snow against the clear
violet sky. And after that it shifted no more. She took
heart now, for at last she seemed to be gaining. Every
laborious step carried her nearer that lofty shining upon
the mountain's highest peak.

She paused after a while, looking up and wiping the
moisture from her forehead where the red curls clung.
As she stood there something among the rocks moved,
and out from behind a boulder a long, slinking feline
creature came. It was not like any beast she had ever
seen before. Its shining pelt was fabulously golden,
brocaded with queer patterns of darker gold, and down
against its heavy jaws curved two fangs whiter than
ivory. With a grace as gliding as water it paced down
the ravine toward her.

Jirel's heart contracted. Somehow she found the
knife-hilt in her hand, though she had no recollection of
having drawn it. She was staring hard at the lovely and
terrible cat, trying to understand the haunting familiarity about its eyes. They were purple, like jewels.
Slowly recognition dawned. She had met that purple
gaze before, insolent under sleepy lids. Jarisme's eyes.
Yes, and the snake in her dream had watched her with a
purple stare too. Jarisme?

She closed her hand tightly about the crystal, knowing that she must conceal from the sorceress her one
potent weapon, waiting until the time came to turn it
against its maker. She shifted her knife so that light
glinted down the blade. They stood quite still for a
moment, yellow-eyed woman and fabulous, purple-
eyed cat, staring at each other with hostility eloquent in
every line of each. Jirel clenched her knife tight, warily

eyeing the steel-clawed paws on which the golden beast went so softly. They could have ripped her to ribbons before the blade struck home.

She saw a queer expression flicker across the somber purple gaze that met hers, and the beautiful cat crouched a little, tail jerking, lip twitched back to expose shining fangs. It was about to spring. For an interminable moment she waited for that hurtling golden death to launch itself upon her, tense, rigid, knife steady in her hand. . . .

It sprang. She dropped to one knee in the split second of its leaping, instinctively hiding the crystal, but thrusting up her dagger in defense. The great beast sailed easily over her head. As it hurtled past, a peal of derisive laughter rang in her ears, and she heard quite clearly the sound of a slamming door. She scrambled up and whirled in one motion, knife ready. The defile was quite empty in the violet day. There was no door anywhere. Jarisme had vanished.

A little shaken, Jirel sheathed her blade. She was not afraid. Anger burned out all trace of fear as she remembered the scorn in that ringing laugh. She took up her course again toward the tower, white and resolute, not looking back.

The tower was drawing near again. She toiled upward. Jarisme showed no further sign of her presence, but Jirel felt eyes upon her, purple eyes, scornful and sleepy. She could see the tower clearly, just above her at the crest of the highest peak, up to which a long arc of steps curved steeply. They were very old, these steps, so worn that many were little more than irregularities on the stone. Jirel wondered what feet had worn them so, to what door they had originally led.

She was panting when she reached the top and peered in under the arch of the door. To her surprise she found herself staring into a broad, semicircular hallway, whose walls were lined with innumerable doors. She remembered the violet nothingness into which she had stepped the last time she crossed the sill, and wondered as she thrust a tentative foot over it if the hall were an illusion and she were really about to plunge once more into that cloudy abyss of falling. But the floor was firm.

She stepped inside and paused, looking round in some bewilderment and wondering where to turn now. She could smell peril in the air. Almost she could taste the magic that hovered like a mist over the whole enchanted place. Little warning prickles ran down her back as she went forward very softly and pushed open one of those innumerable doors. Behind it a gallery stretched down miles of haze-shrouded extent. Arrow-straight it ran, the arches of the ceiling making an endless parade that melted into violet distance. And as she stood looking down the cloudy vista, something like a puff of smoke obscured her vision for an instant—smoke that eddied and billowed and rolled away from the shape of that golden cat which had vanished in the mountain ravine.

It paced slowly down the hall toward her, graceful and lovely, muscles rippling under the brocaded golden coat and purple eyes fixed upon her in a scornful stare. Jirel's hand went to the knife in her belt, hatred choking up in her throat as she met the purple eyes. But in the corridor a voice was echoing softly, Jarisme's voice, saying:

"Then it is war between us, Jirel of Joiry. For you have defied my mercy, and you must be punished. Your punishment I have chosen—the simplest, and the sub-tlest, and the most terrible of all punishments, the worst that could befall a human creature. Can you guess it? No? Then wonder for a while, for I am not prepared yet to administer it fully . . . or shall I kill you now? Eh-h-h? . . .''

The curious, long-drawn query melted into a purring snarl, and the great cat's lip lifted, a flare of murderous light flaming up in the purple eyes. It had been pacing nearer all the while that light voice had echoed in the air. Now its roar crescendoed into a crashing thunder that rang from the walls, and the steel springs of its golden body tightened for a leap straight at Jirel's throat. Scarcely a dozen paces away, she saw the brocaded beauty of it crouching, taut and poised, saw the powerful body quiver and tighten—and spring. In instinctive panic she leaped back and slammed the door in its face.

Derisive laughter belled through the air. A cloud of thin smoke eddied through the crack around the door and puffed in her face with all the insolence of a blow. Then the air was clear again. The red mist of murder swam before Jirel's eyes. Blind with anger, breath beating thickly in her throat, she snatched at the door again, ripping the dagger from her belt. Through that furious haze she glared down the corridor. It was empty. She closed the door a second time and leaned against it, trembling with anger, until the mist had cleared from her head and she could control her shaking hand well enough to replace the dagger.

When she had calmed a little she turned to scan the hall, wondering what to do next. And she saw that there was no escape now, even had she wished, for the door she had entered by was gone. All about her now closed the door-studded walls, enigmatic, imprisoning. And the very fact of their presence was an insult, suggesting that Jarisme had feared she would flee if the entrance were left open. Jirel forced herself into calmness again. She was not afraid, but she knew herself in deadly peril.

She was revolving the sorceress' threat as she cast about for some indication to guide her next step. The simplest and subtlest and most terrible of punishments—what could it be? Jirel knew much of the ways of torture—her dungeons were as blood-stained as any of her neighbors'—but she knew too that Jarisme had not meant only the pain of the flesh. There was a subtler menace in her words. It would be a feminine vengeance, and more terrible than anything iron and fire could inflict. She knew that. She knew also that no door she could open now would lead to freedom, but she could not stay quiet, waiting. She glanced along the rows of dark, identical panels. Anything that magic could contrive might lie behind them. In the face of peril more deadly than death she could not resist the temptation to pull open the nearest one and peer within.

A gust of wind blew in her face and rattled the door. Dust was in that wind, and bitter cold. Through an inner grille of iron, locked across the opening, she saw a dazzle of whiteness like sun on snow in the instant before she slammed the door shut on the piercing gust. But the incident had whetted her curiosity. She moved along the wall and opened another.

This time she was looking through another locked grille into a dimness of gray smoke shot through with flame. The smell of burning rose in her nostrils, and she could hear faintly, as from vast distances, the sound of groans and the shivering echo of screams. Shuddering, she closed the door.

When she opened the next one she caught her breath and stared. Before her a thick crystal door separated her from bottomless space. She pressed her face to the cold glass and stared out and down. Nothingness met her gaze. Dark and silence and the blaze of unwinking stars. It was day outside the tower, but she looked into fathomless night. And as she stared, a long streak of light flashed across the blackness and faded. It was not a shooting star. By straining her eyes she could make out something like a thin sliver of silver flashing across the dark, its flaming tail fading behind it in the sky. And the sight made her ill with sudden vertigo. Bottomless void reeled around her, and she fell back into the hallway, slamming the door upon that terrifying glimpse of starry nothingness.

It was several minutes before she could bring herself to try the next door. When she did, swinging it open timorously, a familiar sweetness of flower perfume floated out and she found herself gazing through a grille of iron bars deep into that drowsy jungle of blossoms and scent and silence which she had crossed at the mountain's foot. A wave of remembrance washed over her. For an instant she could hear those tiny, laughing voices again, and she felt the presence of the great snake at her side, and the wild, mirth-ridden secrets of the little gay voices rang in her ears. Then she was awake again, and the memory vanished as dreams do, leaving nothing but tantalizing fragments of forgotten secrets drifting through her mind. She knew as she stared that she could step straight into that flowery fairyland again if the bars would open. But there was no escape from this magical place, though she might look through any number of opening doors into far lands and near.

She was beginning to understand the significance of the hall. It must be from here that Jarisme by her magical knowledge journeyed into other lands and times and worlds through the doors that opened between her domain and those strange, outland places. Perhaps she had sorcerer friends there, and paid them visits and brought back greater knowledge, stepping from world to world, from century to century, through her enchanted doorways. Jirel felt certain that one of these enigmatic openings would give upon that mountain pass where the golden cat with its scornful purple eyes had sprung at her, and vanished, and laughed backward as the door slammed upon it, and upon the woodland glade where the dryad died. But she knew that bars would close these places away even if she could find them.

She went on with her explorations. One door opened upon a steamy fern-forest of gigantic growths, out of whose deeps floated musky, reptilian odors, and the distant sound of beasts bellowing hollowly. And another upon a gray desert stretching flat and lifeless to the horizon, wan under the light of a dim red sun.

But at last she came to one that opened not into alien lands but upon a stairway winding down into solid rock whose walls showed the mark of the tools that had hollowed them. No sound came up the shaft of the stairs, and a gray light darkened down their silent reaches. Jirel peered in vain for some hint of what lay below. But at last, because inactivity had palled upon her and she knew that all ways were hopeless for escape, she entered the doorway and went slowly down the steps. It occurred to her that possibly she might find Jarisme below, engaged in some obscure magic in the lower regions, and she was eager to come to grips with her enemy.

The light darkened as she descended, until she was groping her way through obscurity round and round the curving stairs. When the steps ended at a depth she could not guess, she could tell that she had emerged into a low-roofed corridor only by feeling the walls and ceiling that met her exploring hands, for the thickest dark hid everything. She made her slow way along the stone hall, which wound and twisted and dipped at unexpected angles until she lost all sense of direction. But she knew she had gone a long way when she began to see the faint gleam of light ahead.

Presently she began to catch the faraway sound of a familiar song—Jarisme's monotonous little flute melody on two notes, and she was sure then that her intuition had been true, that the sorceress was down here somewhere. She drew her dagger in the gloom and went on more warily.

An arched opening ended the passage. Through the arch poured a blaze of dancing white luminance. Jirel paused, blinking and trying to make out what strange place she was entering. The room before her was filled with the baffling glitter and shimmer and mirage of reflecting surfaces so bewilderingly that she could not tell which was real and which mirror, and which dancing light. The brilliance dazzled in her face and dimmed into twilight and blazed again as the mirrors shifted. Little currents of dark shivered through the chaos and brightened into white sparkle once more. That monotonous music came to her through the quivering lights and reflections, now strongly, now faintly in the distance.

The whole place was a chaos of blaze and confusion. She could not know if the room were small or large, a cavern or a palace hall. Queer reflections danced through the dazzle of it. She could see her own image looking back at her from a dozen, a score, a hundred moving planes that grotesquely distorted her and then flickered out again, casting a blaze of light in her blinded eyes. Dizzily she blinked into the reeling wilderness of planes.

Then she saw Jarisme in her violet robe watching her from a hundred identical golden couches reflected upon a hundred surfaces. The figure held a flute to its lips, and the music pulsed from it in perfect time with the pulsing of the sorceress' swelling white throat. Jirel stared round in confusion at the myriad Jarismes all piping the interminable monotones. A hundred sensual, dreamy faces turned to her, a hundred white arms dropped as the flute left a hundred red mouths that Jarisme might smile ironic welcome a hundredfold more scornful for its multiplicity.

When the music ceased, all the flashing dazzle suddenly stilled. Jirel blinked as the chaos resolved itself into shining order, the hundred Jarismes merging into one sleepy-eyed woman lounging upon her golden couch in a vast crystal-walled chamber shaped like the semicircular half of a great, round, domed room. Behind the couch a veil of violet mist hung like a curtain shutting off what would have formed the other half of the circular room.

"Enter," said the sorceress with the graciousness of one who knows herself in full command of the situation. "I thought you might find the way here. I am preparing a ceremony which will concern you intimately. Perhaps you would like to watch? This is to be an experiment, and for that reason a greater honor is to be yours than you can ever have known before; for the company I am assembling to watch your punishment is a more distinguished one than you could understand. Come here, inside the circle."

Jirel advanced, dagger still clenched in one hand, the other closed about her bit of broken crystal. She saw now that the couch stood in the center of a ring engraved in the floor with curious, cabalistic symbols. Beyond it the cloudy violet curtain swayed and eddied within itself, a vast, billowing wall of mist. Dubiously she stepped over the circle and stood eyeing Jarisme, her yellow gaze hot with rigidly curbed emotion. Jarisme smiled and lifted the flute to her lips again.

As the irritating two notes began their seesawing tune Jirel saw something amazing happen. She knew then that the flute was a magic one, and the song magical too. The notes took on a form that overstepped the boundaries of the aural and partook in some inexplicable way of all the other senses too. She could feel them, taste them, smell them, see them. In a queer way they were visible, pouring in twos from the flute and dashing outward like little needles of light. The walls reflected them, and those reflections became swifter and brighter and more numerous until the air was full of flying slivers of silvery brilliance, until shimmers began to dance among them and over them, and that bewildering shift of mirrored planes started up once more. Again reflections crossed and dazzled and multiplied in the shining air as the flute poured out its flashing double notes.

Jirel forgot the sorceress beside her, the music that grated on her ears, even her own peril, in watching the pictures that shimmered and vanished in the mirrored surfaces. She saw flashes of scenes she had glimpsed through the doors of Jarisme's hallway. She saw stranger places than that, passing in instant-brief snatches over the silvery planes. She saw jagged black mountains with purple dawns rising behind them and stars in unknown figures across the dark skies; she saw gray seas flat and motionless beneath gray clouds; she saw smooth meadows rolling horizonward under the glare of double suns. All these and many more awoke to the magic of Jarisme's flute, and melted again to give way to others.

Jirel had the strange fancy, as the music went on, that it was audible in those lands whose brief pictures were flickering across the background of its visible notes. It seemed to be piercing immeasurable distances, ringing across the cloudy seas, echoing under the durable suns, calling insistently in strange lands and far, unknown places, over deserts and mountains that man's feet had never trod, reaching other worlds and other times and crying its two-toned monotony through the darkness of interstellar space. All of this, to Jirel, was no more than a vague realization that it must be so. It meant nothing to her, whose world was a flat plane arched by the heaven-pierced bowl of the sky. Magic, she told herself, and gave up trying to understand.

Presently the tempo of the fluting changed. The same two notes still shrilled endlessly up and down, but it was no longer a clarion call ringing across borderlands into strange worlds. Now it was slower, statelier. And the notes of visible silver that had darted crazily against the crystal walls and reflected back again took on an order that ranked them into one shining plane. Upon that plane Jirel saw the outlines of a familiar scene gradually take shape. The great door-lined hall above mirrored itself in faithful replica before her eyes. The music went on changelessly.

Then, as she watched, one of those innumerable doors quivered. She held her breath. Slowly it swung open upon that gray desert under the red sun which she had seen before she closed it quickly away behind concealing panels. Again as she looked, that sense of utter desolation and weariness and despair came over her, so uncannily dreary was the scene. Now the door stood wide, its locked grille no longer closing it, and as the music went on she could see a dazzle like a jagged twist of lightning begin to shimmer in its aperture. The gleam strengthened. She saw it quiver once, twice, then sweep forward with blinding speed through the open doorway. And as she tried to follow it with her eyes another moving door distracted her.

This time the steamy fern-forest was revealed as the panels swung back. But upon the threshold sprawled something so frightful that Jirel's free hand flew to her lips and a scream beat up in her throat. It was black—shapeless and black and slimy. And it was alive. Like a heap of putrescently shining jelly it heaved itself over the doorsill and began to flow across the floor, inching its way along like a vast blind ameba. But she knew without being told that it was horribly wise, horribly old. Behind it a black trail of slime smeared the floor.

Jirel shuddered and turned her eyes away. Another door was swinging open. Through it she saw a place she had not chanced upon before, a country of bare red rock strewn jaggedly under a sky so darkly blue that it might have been black, with stars glimmering in it more clearly than stars of earth. Across this red, broken desert a figure came striding that she knew could be only a figment of magic, so tall it was, so spidery-thin, so grotesquely human despite its bulbous head and vast chest. She could not see it clearly, for about it like a robe it clutched a veil of blinding light. On those incredibly long, thin legs it stepped across the door-sill, drew its dazzling garment closer about it, and strode forward. As it neared, the light was so blinding that she could not look upon it. Her averted eyes caught the motion of a fourth door.

This time she saw that flowery ravine again, dim in its underwater illusion of diffused light. And out from among the flowers writhed a great serpent-creature, not of the transparent crystal she had seen in her dream, but irridescently scaled. Nor was it entirely serpent, for from the thickened neck sprang a head which could not be called wholly unhuman. The thing carried itself as proudly as a cobra, and as it glided across the threshold its single, many-faceted eye caught Jirel's in the reflection. The eye flashed once, dizzyingly, and she reeled back in sick shock, the violence of that glance burning through her veins like fire. When she regained control of herself many other doors were standing open upon scenes both familiar and strange. During her daze other denizens of those strange worlds must have entered at the call of the magic flute.

She was just in time to see an utterly indescribable thing flutter into the hall from a world which so violated her eyes that she got no more than a glimpse of it as she flung up outraged hands to shut it out. She did not lower that shield until Jarisme's amused voice said in an undertone: "Behold your audience, Jirel of Joiry," and she realized that the music had ceased and a vast silence was pressing against her ears. Then she looked out, and drew a long breath. She was beyond surprise and shock now, and she stared with the dazed incredulity of one who knows herself in a nightmare.

Ranged outside the circle that enclosed the two women sat what was surely the strangest company ever assembled. They were grouped with a queer irregularity which, though meaningless to Jirel, yet gave the impression of definite purpose and design. It had a symmetry so strongly marked that even though it fell outside her range of comprehension she could not but feel the rightness of it.

The light-robed dweller in the red barrens sat there, and the great black blob of shapeless jelly heaved gently on the crystal floor. She saw others she had watched enter, and many more. One was a female creature whose robe of peacock iridescence sprang from her shoulders in great drooping wings and folded round her like a bat's leathery cloak. And her neighbor was a fat gray slug of monster size, palpitating endlessly. One of the crowd looked exactly like a tall white lily swaying on a stalk of silver pallor, but from its chalice poured a light so ominously tinted that she shuddered and turned her eyes away.

Jarisme had risen from her couch. Very tall and regal in her violet robe, she rose against the back-drop of mist which veiled the other half of the room. As she lifted her arms, the incredible company turned to her with an eager expectancy. Jirel shuddered. Then Jarisme's flute spoke softly. It was a different sort of music from the clarion that called them together, from the stately melody which welcomed them through the opening doors. But it harped still on the two seesawing notes, with low, rippling sounds so different from the other two that Jirel marveled at the range of the sorceress' ability on the two notes.

For a few moments as the song went on, nothing happened. Then a motion behind Jarisme caught Jirel's eye. The curtain of violet mist was swaying. The music beat at it and it quivered to the tune. It shook within itself, and paled and thinned, and from behind it a light began to glow. Then on a last low monotone it dissipated wholly and Jirel was staring at a vast globe of quivering light which loomed up under the stupendous arch that soared outward to form the second half of the chamber.

As the last clouds faded she saw that the thing was a huge crystal sphere, rising upon the coils of a translucent purple base in the shape of a serpent. And in the heart of the globe burned a still flame, living, animate, instinct with a life so alien that Jirel stared in utter bewilderment. It was a thing she knew to be alive—yet she knew it could *not* be alive. But she recognized even in her daze of incomprehension its relation to the tiny fragment of crystal she clutched in her hand. In that too the still flame burned. It stung her hand faintly in reminder that she possessed a weapon which could destroy Jarisme, though it might destroy its wielder in the process. The thought gave her a sort of desperate courage.

Jarisme was ignoring her now. She had turned to face the great globe with lifted arms and shining head thrown back. And from her lips a piercingly sweet sound fluted, midway between hum and whistle. Jirel had the wild fancy that she could see that sound arrowing straight into the heart of the vast sphere bulking so high over them all. And in the heart of that still, living flame a little glow of red began to quiver.

Through the trembling air shrilled a second sound. From the corner of her eye Jirel could see that a dark figure had moved forward into the circle and fallen to its knees at the sorceress' side. She knew it for Giraud. Like two blades the notes quivered in the utter hush that lay upon the assembly, and in the globe that red glow deepened.

One by one, other voices joined the chorus, queer, uncanny sounds some of them, from throats not shaped for speech. No two voices blended. The chorus was one of single, unrelated notes. As each voice struck the globe, the fire burned more crimson, until its still pallor had flushed wholly into red. High above the rest soared Jarisme's knife-keen fluting. She lifted her arms higher, and the voices rose in answer. She lowered them, and the blade-like music swooped down an almost visible arc to a lower key. Jirel felt that she could all but see the notes spearing straight from each singer into the vast sphere that dwarfed them all. There was no melody in it, but a sharply definite pattern as alien and unmistakable as the symmetry of their grouping in the room. And as Jarisme's arms rose, lifting the voices higher, the flame burned more deeply red, and paled again as the voices fell.

Three times that stately, violet-robed figure gestured with lifted arms, and three times the living flame deepened and paled. Then Jarisme's voice soared in a high, triumphant cry and she whirled with spread arms, facing the company. In one caught breath, all voices ceased. Silence fell upon them like a blow. Jarisme was no longer priestess, but goddess, as she fronted them in that dead stillness with exultant face and blazing eyes. And in one motion they bowed before her as corn bows under wind. Alien things, shapeless monsters, faceless, eyeless, unrecognizable creatures from unknowable dimensions, abased themselves to the crystal floor before the splendor of light in Jarisme's eyes. For a moment of utter silence the tableau held. Then the sorceress' arms fell.

Ripplingly the company rose. Beyond Jarisme the vast globe had paled again into that living, quiet flame of golden pallor. Immense, brooding, alive, it loomed up above them. Into the strained stillness Jarisme's low voice broke. She was speaking in Jirel's native tongue, but the air, as she went on, quivered thickly with something like waves of sound that were pitched for other organs than human ears. Every word that left her lips made another wave through the thickened air. The assembly shimmered before Jirel's eyes in that broken clarity as a meadow quivers under heat waves.

"Worshippers of the Light," said Jarisme sweetly, "be welcomed from your far dwellings into the presence of the Flame. We who serve it have called you to the worship, but before you return, another sort of ceremony is to be held, which we have felt will interest you all. For we have called it truly the simplest and subtlest and most terrible of all punishments for a human creature.

"It is our purpose to attempt a reversal of this woman's physical and mental self in such a way as to cause her body to become rigidly motionless while her mind—her soul—looks eternally backward along the path it has traveled. You who are human, or have known humanity, will understand what deadly torture that can be. For no human creature, by the laws that govern it, can have led a life whose intimate review is anything but pain. To be frozen into eternal reflections, reviewing all the futility and pain of life, all the pain that thoughtless or intentional acts have caused others, all the spreading consequences of every act—that, to a human being, would be the most dreadful of all torments."

In the silence that fell as her voice ceased, Giraud laid a hand on Jarisme's arm. Jirel saw terror in his eyes.

"Remember," he uttered, "remember, for those who tamper with their known destiny a more fearful thing may come than—"

Jarisme shrugged off the restraining hand impatiently. She turned to Jirel.

"Know, earthling," she said in a queerly strained voice, "that in the books of the future it is written that Jarisme the Sorceress must die at the hands of the one human creature who defies her thrice—and that human creature a woman. Twice I have been weak, and spared you. Once in the forest, once on the roof-top, you cast your puny defiance in my face, and I stayed my hand for fear of what is written. But the third time shall not come. Though you are my appointed slayer, you shall not slay. With my own magic I break Fate's sequence, now, and we shall see!''

In the blaze of her purple eyes Jirel saw that the moment had come. She braced herself, fingers closing about the fragment of crystal in her hand uncertainly as she hesitated, wondering if the time had come for the breaking of her talisman at the sorceress' feet. She hesitated too long, though her waiting was only a split second in duration. For Jarisme's magic was more supremely simple than Jirel could have guessed. The sorceress turned a blazing purple gaze upon her and sharply snapped her plump fingers in the earthwoman's face.

At the sound Jirel's whole world turned inside out about her. It was the sheerest physical agony. Everything vanished as that terrible shift took place. She felt her own body being jerked inexplicably around in a reversal like nothing that any living creature could ever have experienced before. It was a backward-facing in a direction which could have had no existence until that instant. She felt the newness in the second before sight came to her—a breathless, soundless, new-born *now* in which she was the first dweller, created simultaneously with the new plane of being. Then sight broke upon her consciousness.

The thing spread out before her was so stupendous that she would have screamed if she had possessed an animate body. All life was open to her gaze. The sight was too immeasurable for her to grasp it fully—too vast for her human consciousness to look upon at all save in flashing shutter-glimpses without relation or significance. Motion and immobility existed simultaneously in the thing before her. Endless activity shuttling to and fro—yet the whole vast panorama was frozen in a timeless calm through which a mighty pattern ran whose very immensity was enough to strike terror into her soul. Threaded through it the backward trail of her own life stretched. As she gazed upon it such floods of conflicting emotion washed over her that she could not see anything clearly, but she was fiercely insisting to her inner consciousness that she would not—*would not*—look back, dared not, could not—and all the while her sight was running past days and weeks along the path which led inexorably toward the one scene she could not bear to think of.

Very remotely, as her conscious sight retraced the backward way, she was aware of overlapping planes of existence in the stretch of limitless activity before her. Shapes other than human, scenes that had no meaning to her, quivered and shifted and boiled with changing lives—yet lay motionless in the mighty pattern. She scarcely heeded them. For her, of all that panoramic impossibility one scene alone had meaning—the one scene toward which her sight was racing now, do what she would to stop it—the one scene that she knew she could never bear to see again.

Yet when her sight reached that place the pain did not begin at once. She gazed almost calmly upon that little interval of darkness and flaring light, the glare of torches shining upon a girl's bent red head and on a man's long body sprawled motionless upon flagstones.

In the deepest stillness she stared. She felt no urge to look farther, on beyond the scene into the past. This was the climax, the center of all her life—this torch-lit moment on the flagstones. Vividly she was back again in the past, felt the hardness of the cold flags against her knees, and the numbness of her heart as she stared down into a dead man's face. Timelessly she dwelt upon that long-ago heartbreak, and within her something swelled unbearably.

That something was a mounting emotion too great to have name, too complexly blending agony and grief and hatred and love—and rebellion; so strong that all the rest of the stupendous thing before her was blotted out in the gathering storm of what seethed in her innermost consciousness. She was aware of nothing but that overwhelming emotion. And it was boiling into one great unbearable explosion of violence in which rage took precedence over all. Rage at life for permitting such pain to be. Rage at Jarisme for forcing her into memory. Such rage that everything shook before it, and melted and ran together in a heat of rebellion, and— something snapped. The panorama reeled and shivered and collapsed into the dark of semi-oblivion.

Through the clouds of her half-consciousness the agony of change stabbed at her. Half understanding, she welcomed it, though the piercing anguish of that reversal was so strong it dragged her out of her daze again and wrung her anew in the grinding pain of that change which defied all natural laws. In heedless impatience she waited for the torture to pass. Exultation was welling up in her for she knew that her own violence had melted the spell by which Jarisme held her. She knew what she must do when she stood free again, and conscious power flowed intoxicatingly through her.

She opened her eyes. She was standing rigidly before the great fire-quickened globe. The amazing company was grouped around her intently, and Jarisme, facing her, had taken one angry, incredulous step forward as she saw her own spell break. Upon that tableau Jirel's hot yellow eyes opened, and she laughed in grim exultation and swung up her arm. Violet light glinted upon crystal.

In the instant Jarisme saw what she intended, convulsive terror wiped all other expression from her face. A cry of mingled inarticulatenesses thundered up from the transfixed crowd. Giraud started forward from among them, frantic hands clawing out toward her.

"No, no!" shrieked Jarisme. "Wait!"

It was too late. The crystal dashed itself from Jirel's down-swinging arm, the light in it blazing. With a splintering crash it struck the floor at the sorceress's sandaled feet and flew into shining fragments.

For an instant nothing happened. Jirel held her breath, waiting. Giraud had flung himself flat on the shining floor, reaching out for her in a last desperate effort. His hands had flown out to seize her, and found only her ankles. He clung to them now with a paralyzed grip, his face hidden between his arms. Jarisme cowered motionless, arms clasped about her head as if she were trying to hide. The motley throng of watchers was rigid in fatalistic quiet. In tense silence they waited.

Then in the great globe above them the pale flame flickered. Jarisme's gaspingly caught breath sounded loud in the utter quiet. Again the flame shook. And again. Then abruptly it went out. Darkness stunned them for a moment; then a low muttering roar rumbled up out of the stillness, louder and deeper and stronger until it pressed unbearably upon Jirel's ears and her head was one great aching surge of sound. Above that roar a sharply crackling noise broke, and the crystal walls of the room trembled, reeled dizzily—split open in long jagged rents through which the violet day poured in thin fingers of light. Overhead the shattering sound of falling walls roared loud. Jarisme's magic tower was crumbling all around them. Through the long, shivering cracks in the walls the pale violet day poured more strongly, serene in the chaos.

In that clear light Jirel saw a motion among the throng. Jarisme had risen to her full height. She saw the sleek black head go up in an odd, defiant, desperate poise, and above the soul-shaking tumult she heard the sorceress' voice scream:

"Urda! Urda-sla!"

In the midst of the roar of the falling walls for the briefest instant a deathly silence dropped. And out of that silence, like an answer to the sorceress' cry, came a Noise, an indescribable, intolerable loudness like the crack of cyclopean thunder. And suddenly in the sky above them, visible through the crumbling crystal walls, a long black wedge opened. It was like a strip of darkest midnight splitting the violet day, a midnight through which stars shone unbearably near, unbearably bright.

Jirel stared up in dumb surprise at that streak of starry night cleaving the daylit sky. Jarisme stood rigid, arms outstretched, defiantly fronting the thunderous dark whose apex was drawing nearer and nearer, driving downward like a vast celestial spear. She did not flinch as it reached toward the tower. Jirel saw the darkness sweep forward like a racing shadow. Then it was upon them, and the earth shuddered under her feet, and from very far away she heard Jarisme scream.

When consciousness returned to her, she sat up painfully and stared around. She lay upon green grass, bruised and aching, but unharmed. The violet day was serene and unbroken once more. The purple peaks had vanished. No longer was she high among mountains. Instead, the green meadow where she had first seen Jarisme's tower stretched about her. In its dissolution it must have returned to its original site, flashing back along the magical ways it had traveled as the sorceress' magic was broken. For the tower too was gone. A little distance away she saw a heap of marble blocks outlining a rough circle, where that white shaft had risen. But the stones were weathered and cracked like the old, old stones of an ancient ruin.

She had been staring at this for many minutes, trying to focus her bewildered mind upon its significance, before the sound of groaning which had been going on for some time impressed itself on her brain. She turned. A little way off, Giraud lay in a tangle of torn black robes. Of Jarisme and the rest she saw no sign. Painfully she got to her feet and staggered to the wizard, turning him over with a disdainful toe. He opened his eyes and stared at her with a cloudy gaze into which recognition and realization slowly crept.

"Are you hurt?" she demanded.

He pulled himself to a sitting position and flexed his limbs experimentally. Finally he shook his head, more in answer to his own investigation than to her query, and got slowly to his feet. Jirel's eyes sought the weapon at his hip.

"I am going to kill you now," she said calmly. "Draw your sword, wizard."

The little dull eyes flashed up to her face. He stared. Whatever he saw in the yellow gaze must have satisfied him that she meant what she said, but he did not draw, nor did he fall back. A tight little smile drew his mouth askew, and he lifted his black-robed arms. Jirel saw them rise, and her gaze followed the gesture automatically. Up they went, up. And then in the queerest fashion she lost all control of her own eyes, so that they followed some invisible upward line which drew her on and on skyward until she was rigidly staring at a fixed point of invisibility at the spot where the lines of Giraud's arms would have crossed, were they extended to a measureless distance. Somehow she actually saw that point, and could not look away. Gripped in the magic of those lifted arms, she stood rigid, not even realizing what had happened, unable even to think in the moveless magic of Giraud.

His little mocking chuckle reached her from immeasurably far away.

"Kill me?" he was laughing thickly. "Kill me, Giraud? Why, it was you who saved me, Joiry! Why else should I have clung to your ankles so tightly? For I knew that when the Light died, the only one who could hope to live would be the one who slew it—nor was that a certainty, either. But I took the risk, and well I did, or I would be with Jarisme now in the outer dark whence she called up her no-god of the void to save her from oblivion. I warned her what would happen if she tampered with Fate. And I would rather—yes, much rather—be here, in this violet land which I shall rule alone now. Thanks to you, Joiry! Kill me, eh? I think not!''

That thick, mocking chuckle reached her remotely, penetrated her magic-stilled mind. It echoed round and round there, for a long while, before she realized what it meant. But at last she remembered, and her mind woke a little from its inertia, and such anger swept over her that its heat was an actual pain. Giraud, the runaway sorcerer, laughing at Joiry! Holding Jirel of Joiry in his spell! Mocking her! Blindly she wrenched at the bonds of magic, blindly urged her body forward. She could see nothing but that non-existent point where the lifted arms would have crossed, in measureless distances, but she felt the dagger-hilt in her hand, and she lunged forward through invisibility, and did not even know when the blade sank home.

Sight returned to her then in a stunning flood. She rubbed dazed eyes and shook herself and stared round the green meadow in the violet day uncomprehendingly, for her mind was not yet fully awake. Not until she looked down did she remember.

Giraud lay there. The black robes were furled like wings over his quiet body, but red in a thick flood was spreading on the grass, and from the tangled garments her dagger-hilt stood up. Jirel stared down at him, emotionless, her whole body still almost asleep from the power of the dead man's magic. She could not even feel triumph. She pulled the blade free automatically and wiped it on his robes. Then she sat down beside the body and rested her head in her hands, forcing herself to awaken.

After a long while she looked up again, the old hot

light rising in her eyes, life flushing back into her face once more. Shaking off the last shreds of the spell, she got to her feet, sheathing the dagger. About her the violet-misted meadows were very still. No living creature moved anywhere in sight. The trees were motionless in the unstirring air. And beyond the ruins of the marble tower she saw the opening in the woods out of which path had come, very long ago.

Jirel squared her shoulders and turned her back upon her vow fulfilled, and without a backward glance set off across the grass toward the tree-hid ruins which held the gate to home.

The Dark Land

In her great bed in the tower room of Joiry Castle, Jirel of Joiry lay very near to death. Her red hair was a blaze upon the pillow above the bone-whiteness of her face, and the lids lay heavy over the yellow fire of her eyes. Life had gushed out of her in great scarlet spurts from the pike-wound deep in her side, and the whispering women who hovered at the door were telling one another in hushed murmurs that the Lady Jirel had led her last battle charge. Never again would she gallop at the head of her shouting men, swinging her sword with all the ferocity that had given her name such weight among the savage warrior barons whose lands ringed hers. Jirel of Joiry lay very still upon her pillow.

The great two-edged sword which she wielded so recklessly in the heat of combat hung on the wall now where her yellow eyes could find it if they opened, and her hacked and battered armor lay in a heap in one corner of the room just as the women had flung it as they stripped her when the grave-faced men-at-arms came shuffling up the stairs bearing the limp form of their lady, heavy in her mail. The room held the hush of death. Nothing in it stirred. On the bed Jirel's white face lay motionless among the pillows.

Presently one of the women moved forward and gently pulled the door to against their watching.

"It is unseemly to stare so," she reproved the others. "Our lady would not desire us to behold her thus until Father Gervase has shriven her sins away."

And the coifed heads nodded assent, murmurous among themselves. In a moment or two more a commotion on the stairs forced the massed watchers apart, and Jirel's serving-maid came up the steps holding a kerchief to her reddened eyes and leading Father Gervase. Someone pushed open the door for them, and the crowd parted to let them through.

The serving-maid stumbled forward to the bedside, mopping her eyes blindly. Behind her something obscurely wrong was happening. After a moment she realized what it was. A great stillness had fallen stunningly upon the crowd. She lifted a bewildered gaze toward the door. Gervase was staring at the bed in the blankest amazement.

"My child," he stammered, "where is your lady?"

The girl's head jerked round toward the bed. It was empty.

The sheets still lay exactly as they had covered Jirel, not pushed back as one pushes the blankets on arising. The hollow where her body had lain still held its shape among the yet warm sheets, and no fresh blood spattered the floor; but of the Lady of Joiry there was no sign.

Gervase's hands closed hard on his silver crucifix

and under the fringe of gray hair his face crumpled suddenly into grief.

"Our dear lady has dabbled too often in forbidden things," he murmured to himself above the crucifix. "Too often. . . ."

Behind him trembling hands signed the cross, and awed whispers were already passing the word back down the crowded stairs: "The devil himself has snatched Jirel of Joiry body and soul out of her death-bed."

Jirel remembered shouts and screams and the din of battle, and that stunning impact in her side. Afterward nothing but dimness floating thickly above a bedrock of savage pain, and the murmur of voices from very far away. She drifted bodiless and serene upon a dark tide that was ebbing seaward, pulling her out and away while the voices and the pain receded to infinite distances, and faded and ceased.

Then somewhere a light was shining. She fought the realization weakly, for the dark tide pulled seaward and her soul desired the peace it seemed to promise with a longing beyond any words to tell. But the light would not let her go. Rebellious, struggling, at last she opened her eyes. The lids responded sluggishly, as if they had already forgotten obedience to her will. But she could see under the fringe of lashes, and she lay motionless, staring quietly while life flowed back by slow degrees into the body it had so nearly left.

The light was a ring of flames, leaping golden against the dark beyond them. For a while she could see no more than that circlet of fire. Gradually perception returned behind her eyes, and reluctantly the body that had hovered so near to death took up the business of living again. With full comprehension she stared, and as she realized what it was she looked upon, incredulity warred with blank amazement in her dazed mind.

Before her a great image sat, monstrous and majestic upon a throne. Throne and image were black and shining. The figure was that of a huge man, wide-shouldered, tremendous, many times life size. His face was bearded, harsh with power and savagery, and very regal, haughty as Lucifer's might have been. He sat upon his enormous black throne staring arrogantly into nothingness. About his head the flames were leaping. She looked harder, unbelieving. How could she have come here? What was it, and where? Blank-eyed, she stared at that flaming crown that circled the huge head, flaring and leaping and casting queer bright shadows over the majestic face below them.

Without surprise, she found that she was sitting up. In her stupor she had not known the magnitude of her hurt, and it did not seem strange to her that no pain attended the motion, or that her pike-torn side was whole again beneath the doeskin tunic which was all she wore. She could not have known that the steel point of the pike had driven the leather into her flesh so deeply that her women had not dared to remove the garment lest they open the wound afresh and their lady die before absolution came to her. She only knew that she sat here naked in her doeskin tunic, her bare feet on a fur rug and cushions heaped about her. And all this was so strange and inexplicable that she made no attempt to understand.

The couch on which she sat was low and broad and black, and that fur rug in whose richness her toes were rubbing luxuriously was black too, and huger than any beast's pelt could be outside dreams.

Before her, across an expanse of gleaming black floor the mighty image rose, crowned with flame. For the rest, this great, black, dim-lighted room was empty. The flame-reflections danced eerily in the shining floor. She lifted her eyes, and saw with a little start of surprise that there was no ceiling. The walls rose immensely overhead, terminating in jagged abruptness above which a dark sky arched, sown with dim stars.

This much she had seen and realized before a queer glittering in the air in front of the image drew her roving eyes back. It was a shimmer and dance like the dance of dust motes in sunshine, save that the particles which glittered in the darkness were multicolored, dazzling. They swirled and swarmed before her puzzled eyes in a queer dance that was somehow taking shape in the light of the flames upon the image's head. A figure was forming in the midst of the rainbow shimmer. A man's figure, a tall, dark-visaged, heavy-shouldered man whose outlines among the dancing motes took on rapid form and solidarity, strengthening by moments until in a last swirl the gaily colored dazzle dissipated and the man himself stood wide-legged before her, fists planted on his hips, grinning darkly down upon the spellbound Jirel.

He was the image. Save that he was of flesh and blood, life size, and the statue was of black stone and gigantic, there was no difference. The same harsh, arrogant, majestic face turned its grim smile upon Jirel. From under scowling black brows, eyes that glittered blackly with little red points of intolerable brilliance blazed down upon her. She could not meet that gaze. A short black beard outlined the harshness of his jaw, and through it the white flash of his smile dazzled her.

This much about the face penetrated even Jirel's dazed amazement, and she caught her breath in a sudden gasp, sitting up straighter among her cushions and staring. The dark stranger's eyes were eager upon the long, lithe lines of her upon the couch. Red sparkles quickened in their deeps, and his grin widened.

"Welcome," he said, in a voice so deep and rich that involuntarily a little burr of answer rippled along Jirel's nerves. "Welcome to the dark land of Romne."

"Who brought me here?" Jirel found her voice at last. "And why?"

"I did it," he told her. "I—Pav, king of Romne. Thank me for it, Jirel of Joiry. But for Pav you had lain among the worms tonight. It was out of your death-bed I took you, and no power but mine could have mended the pike-hole in your side or put back into you the blood you spilled on Triste battlefield. Thank me, Jirel!"

She looked at him levelly, her yellow eyes kindling a little in rising anger as she met the laughter in his.

"Tell me why you brought me here."

At that he threw back his head and laughed hugely, a bull bellow of savage amusement that rang in deep echoes from the walls and beat upon her ears with the sound of organ notes. The room shook with his laughter; the little flames around the image's head danced to it.

"To be my bride, Joiry!" he roared. "That look of defiance ill becomes you, Jirel! Blush, lady, before your bridegroom!"

The blankness of the girl's amazement was all that saved her for the moment from the upsurge of murderous fury which was beginning to seethe below the surface of her consciousness. She could only stare as he laughed down at her, enjoying to the full her mute amaze.

"Yes," he said at last, "you have traveled too often in forbidden lands, Jirel of Joiry, to be ignored by us who live in them. And there is in you a hot and savage strength which no other woman in any land I know possesses. A force to match my own, Lady Jirel. None but you is fit to be my queen. So I have taken you for my own."

Jirel gasped in a choke of fury and found her voice again.

"Hell-dwelling madman!" she spluttered. "Black beast out of nightmares! Let me waken from this crazy dream!"

"It is no dream," he smiled infuriatingly. "As you died in Joiry Castle I seized you out of your bed and snatched you body and soul over the space-curve that parts this land from yours. You have awakened in your own dark kingdom, O Queen of Romne!" And he swept her an ironical salute, his teeth glittering in the darkness of his beard.

"By what right—" blazed Jirel.

"By a lover's right," he mocked her. "Is it not better to share Romne with me than to reign among the worms, my lady? For death was very near to you just now. I have saved your lovely flesh from a cold bed, Jirel, and kept your hot soul rooted there for you. Do I get no thanks for that?"

Yellow fury blazed in her eyes.

"The thanks of a sword-edge, if I had one," she flared. "Do you think to take Joiry like some peasant wench to answer to your whims? I'm Joiry, man! You must be mad!''

"I'm Pav," he answered her somberly, all mirth vanishing in a breath from his heavy voice. "I'm king of Romne and lord of all who dwell therein. For your savageness I chose you, but do not try me too far, Lady Jirel!"

She looked up into the swart, harsh face staring down on her, and quite suddenly the nearest thing she had ever known to fear of a human being came coldly over her; perhaps the fear that if any man alive could tame her fierceness, this man could. The red prickles had gone out of his eyes, and something in her shuddered a little from that black, unpupiled stare. She veiled the hawk-yellow of her own gaze and set her lips in a straight line.

"I shall call your servants," said Pav heavily. "You must be clothed as befits a queen, and then I shall show you your land of Romne."

She saw the black glare of his eyes flick sidewise as if in search, and in the instant his gaze sought them there appeared about her in the empty air the most curious phenomenon she had ever seen. Queer, shimmering bluenesses swarm shoulder-high all around her, blue and translucent like hot flames, and like flames their outlines flickered. She never saw them clearly, but their touch upon her was like the caress a flame might give if it bore no heat: swift, brushing, light.

All about her they seethed, moving too quickly for the eyes to follow; all over her the quick, flickering caresses ran. And she felt queerly exhausted as they moved, as if strength were somehow draining out of her while the blue flames danced. When their bewildering ministrations ceased the strange weariness abated too, and Jirel in blank surprise looked down at her own long, lovely body sheathed in the most exquisite velvet she had ever dreamed of. It was black as a starless night, softer than down, rich and lustrous as it molded her shining curves into sculptured beauty. There was a sensuous delight in the soft swirl of it around her feet as she moved, in the dark caress of it upon her flesh when motion stirred the silken surfaces against her skin. For an instant she was lost in pure feminine ecstasy.

But that lasted only for an instant. Then she heard Pav's deep voice saying: "Look!" and she lifted her eyes to a room whose outlines were melting away like smoke. The great image faded, the gleaming floor and the jagged, roofless walls turned translucent and misty, and through their melting surfaces mountains began to loom in the distance, dark trees and rough, uneven land. Before the echoes of Pav's deeply vibrant "Look!" had shivered wholly into silence along her answering nerves, the room had vanished and they two stood alone in the midst of the dark land of Romne.

It was a dark land indeed. As far as she could see, the air swallowed up every trace of color, so that in somber grays and blacks the landscape stretched away under her eyes. But it had a curious clarity, too, in the dark, translucent air. She could see the distant mountains black and clear beyond the black trees. Beyond them, too, she caught a gleam of still black water, and under her feet the ground was black and rocky. And there was a curiously circumscribed air about the place. Somehow she felt closed in as she stared, for the horizon seemed nearer than it should be, and its dark circle bound the little world of grayness and blackness and clear, dark air into a closeness she could not account for.

She felt prisoned in and a little breathless, for all the wide country spreading so clearly, so darkly about her. Perhaps it was because even out at the far edge of the sky everything was as distinct in the transparent darkness of the air as the rocks at her very feet, so that there was no sense of distance here at all.

Yes, it was a dark land, and a strange land, forbidding, faintly nightmarish in the color-swallowing clarity of its air, the horizons too near and too clear in the narrowness of their circle.

"This," said Pav beside her, in his nerve-tingling voice that sent unconquerable little shudders of answer along her resounding nerves, "this is your land of Romne, O Queen! A land wider than it looks, and one well befitted to your strength and loveliness, my Jirel. A strange land, too, by all earthly standards. Later you must learn how strange. The illusion of it—"

"Save your breath, King of Romne," Jirel broke in upon his deep-voiced speech. "This is no land of mine, and holds no interest for me save in its way out. Show me the gate back into my own world, and I shall be content never to see Romne or you again."

Pav's big hand shot out and gripped her shoulder ungently. He swung her round in a swirl of velvet skirts and a toss of fire-colored hair, and his dark, bearded face was savage with anger. The little red dazzles danced in his unpupiled black eyes until she could not focus her own hot yellow gaze upon them, and dropped her eyes from his in helpless fury.

"You are mine!" he told her in a voice so deep and low that her whole body tingled to its vibration. "I took you out of Joiry and your death-bed and the world you knew, and you are mine from this moment on. Strong you may be, but not so strong as I, Jirel of Joiry, and when I command, henceforth obey!''

Blind with fury, Jirel ripped his hand away and fell back one step in a swirl of black skirts. She tossed her head up until the curls upon it leaped like flames, and the scorching anger in her voice licked up in matching flames, so hotly that her speech was broken and breathless as she choked in a half-whisper.

''Never touch me again, you black hell-dweller! Before God, you'd never have dared if you'd left me a knife to defend myself with! I swear I'll tear the eyes out of your head if I feel the weight of your hand on me again! Yours, you filthy wizard? You'll never have me—never, if I must die to escape you! By my name I swear it!''

She choked into silence, not for lack of words but because the mounting fury that seethed up in her throat drowned out all further sound. Her eyes were blazing yellow with scorching heat, and her fingers flexed like claws eager for blood.

The King of Romne grinned down at her, thumbs hooked in his belt and derision gleaming whitely in the whiteness of his smile. The little beard jutted along his jaw, and red lights were flickering in the fathomless darkness of his eyes.

''You think so, eh, Joiry!'' he mocked her, deep-voiced. ''See what I *could* do!''

He did not shift a muscle, but even through her blinding fury she was aware of a sudden altering in him, a new power and command. His red-gleaming eyes were hot upon hers, and with sick anger she realized anew that she could not sustain that gaze. There was something frightening in the unpupiled blackness of it, the blazing, unbearable strength that beat out from it in heavy command. It was a command all out of proportion to his moveless silence, a command that wrenched at her intolerably. She must obey—she must. . . .

Suddenly a fresh wave of soul-scorching heat surged over her blindingly, terribly, in such a burst that the whole dark land of Romne blazed into nothingness and she lost all grip upon reality. The rocky ground swirled sidewise and vanished. The dark world dissolved around her. She was not flesh and blood but a white-hot incandescence of pure rage. Through the furnace heat of it, as through a shimmer of flame, she saw the body that her own violence had wrenched her out of. It stood straight in its gown of velvety blackness, facing Pav's unmoving figure defiantly. But as she watched, a weakening came over it. The stiffness went out of its poise, the high red head drooped. Helplessly she watched her own forsaken body moving forward step by reluctant step, as if the deserted flesh itself resented the subjection so forced upon it. She saw herself come to Pav's feet. She saw her black-sheathed body bend submissively, ripple pliantly to its knees. In a stillness beyond any ultimate climax of incarnate fury, she saw herself abased before Pav, her head bowed, her body curving into lines of warm surrender at his feet.

And she was afraid. For from somewhere a power was beating of such intolerable magnitude that even the inferno of her fury was abashed before it. Her body's obedience lost all significance in the rush of that terrible force. She would have thought that it radiated from Pav had it been possible for any human creature to sustain such an incredible force as that she was so fleetingly aware of.

For the briefest instant the knowledge of that power was all around her, terrifyingly, thunderously. It was too tremendous a thing to endure in her state of un-bodied vulnerability. It scorched her like strong flame. And she was afraid—for Pav was the center of that inferno's might, and he could be no human thing who radiated such an infinity of power. What was he? What *could* he be—?

In that instant she was horribly afraid—soul-naked in the furnace blast of something too tremendous . . . too terrible. . . .

Then the moment of separation ceased. With a rush and a dazzle she was back in her kneeling body, and the knowledge of that power faded from about her and the humiliation of her pose burned again hotly in her throat. Like a spring released she leaped to her feet, starting back and blazing into Pav's smiled face so hotly that her whole body seemed incandescent with the rage that flooded back into it. That moment of terror was fuel to feed the blaze, for she was not naked now, not bodiless and undefended from the force she had so briefly sensed, and anger that she had been exposed to it, that she had felt terror of it, swelled with the fury of her abasement before Pav. She turned eyes like two pits of hell-blaze upon her tormentor. But before she could speak:

"I admit your power," said Pav in a somewhat surprised voice. "I could conquer your body thus, but only by driving out the blaze that is yourself. I have never known before a mortal creature so compounded that my will could not conquer his. It proves you a fit mate for Pav of Romne. But though I could force you to my command, I shall not. I desire no woman against her will. You are a little human thing, Jirel, and your fullest strength against mine is like a candle in the sun—but in these last few minutes I have learned respect for you. Will you bargain with me?''

''I'd bargain sooner with the Devil,'' she whispered hotly. ''Will you let me go, or must I die to be free?''

Somberly he looked down at her. The smile had vanished from his bearded mouth, and a dark majesty was brooding upon the swarthy face turned down to hers. His eyes flashed red no longer. They were black with so deep a blackness that they seemed two holes of fathomless space, two windows into infinity. To look into them sent something in Jirel sick with sudden vertigo. Somehow, as she stared, her white-blazing fury cooled a little. Again she felt subtly that here was no human thing into whose eyes she gazed. A quiver of fright struggled up through her fading anger. At last he spoke.

''What I take I do not lightly give up. No, there is in you a heady violence that I desire, and will not surrender. But I do not wish you against your will.''

''Give me a chance then, at escape,'' said Jirel. Her boiling anger had died almost wholly away under his somber, dizzying gaze, in the memory of that instant when inferno itself had seemed to beat upon her from the power of his command. But there had not abated in her by any fraction of lessening purpose the determination not to yield. Indeed, she was strengthened against him by the very knowledge of his more than human power—the thing which in her unbodied nakedness had burned like a furnace blast against the defenseless soul

of her was terrible enough even in retrospect to steel all
her resolution against surrender. She said in a steady
voice:

"Let me seek through your land of Romne the gateway back into my own world. If I fail—"

"You cannot but fail. There is no gateway by which
you could pass."

"I am unarmed," she said desperately, grasping at
straws in her determination to find some excuse to leave
him. "You have taken me helpless and weaponless into
your power, and I shall not surrender. Not until you
have shown yourself my master—and I do not think you
can. Give me a weapon and let me prove that!"

Pav smiled down on her as a man smiles on a rebellious child.

"You have no idea what you ask," he said. "I am
not"—he hesitated—"perhaps not wholly as I seem to
you. Your greatest skill could not prevail against me."

"Then let me find a weapon!" Her voice trembled a
little with the anxiety to be free of him, to find somehow
an escape from the intolerable blackness of his eyes, the
compulsion of his presence. For every moment that
those terrible eyes beat so hotly upon her she felt her
resistance weaken more, until she knew that if she did
not leave him soon all strength would melt away in her
and her body of its own will sink once more into
surrender at his feet. To cover her terror she blustered,
but her voice was thick. "Give me a weapon! There is
no man alive who is not somehow vulnerable. I shall
learn your weakness, Pav of Romne, and slay you with
it. And if I fail—then take me."

The smile faded slowly from Pav's bearded lips. He
stood in silence, looking down at her, and the fathom-

less darkness of his eyes radiated power like heat in
such insupportable strength that her own gaze fell before it and she stared down at her velvet shirt-hem on
the rocks. At last he said:

"Go, then. If that will content you, seek some means
to slay me. But when you fail, remember—you have
promised to acknowledge me your lord."

"If I fail!" Relief surged up in Jirel's throat. *"If* I
fail!"

He smiled again briefly, and then somehow all about
his magnificent dark figure a swirl of rainbow dazzle
was dancing. She stared, half afraid, half in awe,
watching the tall, black tangibility of him melting easily into that multicolored whirling she had seen before,
until nothing was left but the dazzling swirl that slowed
and faded and dissipated upon the dark air—and she
was alone.

She drew a deep breath as the last of the rainbow
shimmer faded into nothing. It was a heavenly relief not
to feel the unbearable power of him beating unceasingly
against her resistance, not to keep tense to the
breaking-point all the strength that was in her. She
turned away from the spot where he had vanished and
scanned the dark land of Romne, telling herself resolutely that if she found no gateway, no weapon, then
death itself must open the way out of Romne. There was
about Pav's terrible strength something that set the
nerves of her humanity shuddering against it. In her
moment of soul-nakedness she had sensed that too fully
ever to surrender. The inferno of the *thing* that was Pav
burning upon her unbodied consciousness had been the
burning of something so alien that she knew with every
instinct in her that she would die if she must, rather than

submit. Pav's body was the body of a man, but it was not—she sensed it intuitively—as a man alone that he desired her, and from surrender to the dark intensity of what lay beyond the flesh her whole soul shuddered away.

She looked about helplessly. She was standing upon stones, her velvet skirts sweeping black jagged rock that sloped down toward the distant line of trees. She could see the shimmer of dark water between them, and above and beyond their swaying tops the black mountains loomed. Nowhere was there any sign of the great chamber where the image sat. Nowhere could she see anything but deserted rocks, empty meadows, trees where no birds sang. Over the world of grayness and blackness she stood staring.

And again she felt that sense of imprisonment in the horizon's dark, close bounds. It was a curiously narrow land, this Romne. She felt it intuitively, though there was no visible barrier closing her in. In the clear, dark air even the mountains' distant heights were distinct and colorless and black.

She faced them speculatively, wondering how far away their peaks lay. A dark thought was shadowing her mind, for it came to her that if she found no escape from Romne and from Pav the mountains alone offered that final escape which she was determined to take if she must. From one of those high, sheer cliffs she could leap. . . .

It was not tears that blurred the black heights suddenly. She stared in bewilderment, lifted dazed hands to rub her eyes, and then stared again. Yes, no mistake about it, the whole panorama of the land of Romne was melting like mist about her. The dark trees with their glint of lake beyond, the rocky foreground, everything faded and thinned smokily, while through the vanishing contours those far mountains loomed up near and clear overhead. Dizzy with incomprehension, she found herself standing amid the shreds of dissipating landscape at the very foot of those mountains which a moment before had loomed high and far on the edge of the horizon. Pav had been right indeed—Romne was a strange land. What had he said—about the illusion of it?

She looked up, trying to remember, seeing the dark slopes tilting over her head. High above, on a ledge of outcropping stone, she could see gray creepers dropping down the rocky sides, the tips of tall trees waving. She stared upward toward the ledge whose face she could not see, wondering what lay beyond the vine-festooned edges. And:

In a thin, dark fog the mountainside melted to her gaze. Through it, looming darkly and more darkly as the fog thinned, a level plateau edged with vines and thick with heavy trees came into being before her. She stood at the very edge of it, the dizzy drop of the mountain falling sheer behind her. By no path that feet can tread could she have come to this forested plateau.

One glance she cast backward and down from her airy vantage above the dark land of Romne. It spread out below her in a wide horizon-circle of black rock and black waving tree-tops and colorless hills, clear in the clear, dark air of Romne. Nowhere was anything but rock and hills and trees, clear and distinct out to the horizon in the color-swallowing darkness of the air. No sight of man's occupancy anywhere broke the somberness of its landscape. The great black hall where the image burned might never have existed save in dreams. A prison land it was, narrowly bound by the tight circle of the sky.

Something insistent and inexplicable tugged at her attention then, breaking off abruptly that scanning of the land below. Not understanding why, she answered the compulsion to turn. And when she had turned she stiffened into rigidity, one hand halting in a little futile reach after the knife that no longer swung at her side; for among the trees a figure was approaching.

It was a woman—or could it be? White as leprosy against the blackness of the trees, with a whiteness that no shadows touched, so that she seemed like some creature out of another world reflecting in dazzling pallor upon the background of the dark, she paced slowly forward. She was thin—deathly thin, and wrapped in a white robe like a winding-sheet. The black hair lay upon her shoulders as snakes might lie.

But it was her face that caught Jirel's eyes and sent a chill of sheer terror down her back. It was the face of Death itself, a skull across which the white, white flesh was tightly drawn. And yet it was not without a certain stark beauty of its own, the beauty of bone so finely formed that even in its death's-head nakedness it was lovely.

There was no color upon that face anywhere. White-lipped, eyes shadowed, the creature approached with a leisured swaying of the long robe, a leisured swinging of the long black hair lying in snake-strands across the thin white shoulders. And the nearer the—the woman?—came the more queerly apart from the land about her she seemed. Bone-white, untouched by any shadow save in the sockets of her eyes, she was shockingly detached from even the darkness of the air. Not all of Romne's dim, color-veiling atmosphere could mask the staring whiteness of her, almost blinding in its unshadowed purity.

As she came nearer, Jirel sought instinctively for the eyes that should be fixed upon her from those murky hollows in the scarcely fleshed skull. If they were there, she could not see them. An obscurity clouded the dim sockets where alone shadows clung, so that the face was abstract and sightless—not blind, but more as if the woman's thoughts were far away and intent upon something so absorbing that her surroundings held nothing for the hidden eyes to dwell on.

She paused a few paces from the waiting Jirel and stood quietly, not moving. Jirel had the feeling that from behind those shadowy hollows where the darkness clung like cobwebs a close and critical gaze was analyzing her, from red head to velvet-hidden toes. At last the bloodless lips of the creature parted and from them a voice as cool and hollow as a tomb fell upon Jirel's ears in queer, reverberating echoes, as if the woman spoke from far away in deep caverns underground, coming in echo upon echo out of the depths of unseen vaults, though the air was clear and empty about her. Just as her shadowless whiteness gave the illusion of a reflection from some other world, so the voice seemed also to come from echoing distances. Its hollowness said slowly:

"So here is the mate Pav chose. A red woman, eh? Red as his own flame. What are you doing here, bride, so far from your bridegroom's arms?"

"Seeking a weapon to slay him with!" said Jirel hotly. "I am not a woman to be taken against her will, and Pav is no choice of mine."

Again she felt that hidden scrutiny from the pits of the veiled eyes. When the cool voice spoke it held a note of incredulity that sounded clearly even in the hollowness of its echo from the deeps of invisible tombs.

"Are you mad? Do you not know what Pav is? You actually seek to *destroy* him?"

"Either him or myself," said Jirel angrily. "I know only that I shall never yield to him, whatever he may be."

"And you came—here. Why? How did you know? How did you dare?" The voice faded and echoes whispered down vaults and caverns of unseen depth ghostily, "—did you dare—did you dare—you dare. . . ."

"Dare what?" demanded Jirel uneasily. "I came here because—because when I gazed upon the mountains, suddenly the world dissolved around me and I was—was here."

This time she was quite sure that a long, deep scrutiny swept her from head to feet, boring into her eyes as if it would read her very thoughts, though the cloudy pits that hid the woman's eyes revealed nothing. When her voice sounded again it held a queer mingling of relief and amusement and stark incredulity as it reverberated out of its hollow, underground places.

"Is this ignorance or guile, woman? Can it be that you do not understand even the secret of the land of Romne, or why, when you gazed at the mountains, you found yourself here? Surely even you must not have imagined Romne to be—as it seems. Can you possibly have come here unarmed and alone, to my very mountain—to my very grove—to my very face? You say you seek destruction?'' The cool voice murmured into laughter that echoed softly from unseen walls and caverns in diminishing sounds, so that when the woman spoke again it was to the echoes of her own fading mirth. ''How well you have found your way! Here is death for you—here at my hands! For you must have known that I shall surely kill you!''

Jirel's heart leaped thickly under her velvet gown. Death she had sought, but not death at the hands of such a thing as this. She hesitated for words, but curiosity was stronger even than her sudden jerk of reflexive terror, and after a moment she contrived to ask, in a voice of rigid steadiness:

''Why?''

Again the long, deep scrutiny from eyeless sockets. Under it Jirel shuddered, somehow not daring to take her gaze from that leprously white, skull-shaped face, though the sight of it sent little shivers of revulsion along her nerves. Then the bloodless lips parted again and the cool, hollow voice fell echoing on her ears:

''I can scarcely believe that you do not know. Surely Pav must be wise enough in the ways of women—even such as I—to know what happens when rivals meet. No, Pav shall not see his bride again, and the white witch will be queen once more. Are you ready for death, Jirel of Joiry?''

The last words hung hollowly upon the dark air, echoing and re-echoing from invisible vaults. Slowly the arms of the corpse-creature lifted, trailing the white robe in great pale wings, and the hair stirred upon her shoulders like living things. It seemed to Jirel that a light was beginning to glimmer through the shadows that clung like cobwebs to the skullface's sockets, and somehow she knew chokingly that she could not bear to gaze upon what was dawning there if she must throw herself backward off the cliff to escape it. In a voice that strangled with terror she cried:

"Wait!"

The pale-winged arms hesitated in their lifting; the light which was dawning behind the shadowed eye-sockets for a moment ceased to brighten through the veiling. Jirel plunged on desperately:

"There is no need to slay me. I would very gladly go if I knew the way out."

"No," the cold voice echoed from reverberant distances. "There would be the peril of you always, existing and waiting. No, you must die or my sovereignty is at an end."

"Is it sovereignty or Pav's love that I peril, then?" demanded Jirel, the words tumbling over one another in her breathless eagerness lest unknown magic silence her before she could finish.

The corpse-witch laughed a cold little echo of sheer scorn.

"There is no such thing as love," she said, "—for such as I."

"Then," said Jirel quickly, a feverish hope beginning to rise behind her terror, "then let me be the one to slay. Let me slay Pav as I set out to do, and leave this land kingless, for your rule alone."

For a dreadful moment the half-lifted arms of the figure that faced her so terribly hesitated in midair; the light behind the shadows of her eyes flickered. Then slowly the winged arms fell, the eyes dimmed into cloud-filled hollows again. Blind-faced, impersonal, the skull turned toward Jirel. And curiously, she had the idea that calculation and malice and a dawning idea that spelled danger for her were forming behind that expressionless mask of white-fleshed bone. She could feel tensity and peril in the air—a subtler danger than the frank threat of killing. Yet when the white witch spoke there was nothing threatening in her words. The hollow voice sounded as coolly from its echoing caverns as if it had not a moment before been threatening death.

"There is only one way in which Pav can be destroyed," she said slowly. "It is a way I dare not attempt, nor would any not already under the shadow of death. I think not even Pav knows of it. If you—" The hollow tones hesitated for the briefest instant, and Jirel felt, like the breath of a cold wind past her face, the certainty that there was a deeper danger here, in this unspoken offer, than even in the witch's scarcely stayed death-magic. The cool voice went on, with a tingle of malice in its echoing.

"If you dare risk this way of clearing my path to the throne of Romne, you may go free."

Jirel hesitated, so strong had been that breath of warning to the danger-accustomed keenness of her senses. It was not a genuine offer—not a true path of escape. She was sure of that, though she could not put her finger on the flaw she sensed so strongly. But she knew she had no choice.

"I accept, whatever it is," she said, "my only hope of winning back to my own land again. What is this thing you speak of?"

"The—the flame," said the witch half hesitantly,

and again Jirel felt a sidelong scrutiny from the cob-webbed sockets, almost as if the woman scarcely expected to be believed. "The flame that crowns Pav's image. If it can be quenched, Pav—dies." And queerly she laughed as she said it, a cool little ripple of scornful amusement. It was somehow like a blow in the face, and Jirel felt the blood rising to her cheeks as if in answer to a tangible slap. For she knew that the scorn was directed at herself, though she could not guess why.

"But how?" she asked, striving to keep bewilderment out of her voice.

"With flame," said the white witch quickly. "Only with flame can that flame be quenched. I think Pav must at least once have made use of those little blue fires that flicker through the air about your body. Do you know them?"

Jirel nodded mutely.

"They are the manifestations of your own strength, called up by him. I can explain it no more clearly to you than that. You must have felt a momentary exhaustion as they moved. But because they are essentially a part of your own human violence, here in this land of Romne, which is stranger and more alien than you know, they have the ability to quench Pav's flame. You will not understand that now. But when it happens, you will know why. I cannot tell you.

"You must trick Pav into calling forth the blue fire of your own strength, for only he can do that. And then you must concentrate all your forces upon the flame that burns around the image. Once it is in existence, you can control the blue fire, send it out to the image. You must do this. Will you? Will you?"

The tall figure of the witch leaned forward eagerly, her white skull-face thrusting nearer in an urgency that not even the veiled, impersonal eye-sockets could keep from showing. And though she had imparted the information that the flame held Pav's secret life in a voice of hollow reverberant mockery, as if the statement were a contemptuous lie, she told of its quenching with an intensity of purpose that proclaimed it unmistakable truth. "Will you?" she demanded again in a voice that shook a little with nameless violence.

Jirel stared at the white-fleshed skull in growing disquiet. There was a danger here that she could feel almost tangibly. And somehow it centered upon this thing which the corpse-witch was trying to force her into promising. Somehow she was increasingly sure of that. And rebellion suddenly flamed within her. If she must die, then let her do it now, meeting death face to face and not in some obscurity of cat's-paw witchcraft in the attempt to destroy Pav. She would not promise.

"No," she heard her own voice saying in sudden violence. "No, I will not!"

Across the skull-white face of the witch convulsive fury swept. It was the rage of thwarted malice, not the disappointment of a plotter. The hollow voice choked behind grinning lips, but she lifted her arms like great pale wings again, and a glare of hell-fire leaped into being among the shadows that clung like cobwebs to her eye-sockets. For a moment she stood towering, white and terrible, above the earthwoman, in a tableau against the black woods of unshadowed bone-whiteness, dazzling in the dark air of Romne, terrible beyond words in the power of her gathering magic.

Then Jirel, rigid with horror at the light brightening

so ominously among the shadows of these eyeless
sockets, saw terror sweep suddenly across the convulsed face, quenching the anger in a cold tide of deadly
fear.

"Pav!" gasped the chill voice hollowly. "Pav
comes!"

Jirel swung round toward the far horizon, seeking
what had struck such fear into the leprously white
skull-face, and with a little gasp of reprieve saw the
black figure of her abductor enormous on the distant
skyline. Through the clear dark air she could see him
plainly, even to the sneering arrogance upon his
bearded face, and a flicker of hot rebellion went
through her. Even in the knowledge of his black and
terrible power, the human insolence of him struck
flame from the flint of her resolution, and she began to
burn with a deep-seated anger which not even his terror
could quench, not even her amazement at the incredible
size of him.

For he strode among the tree-tops like a colossus,
gigantic, heaven-shouldering, swinging in league-long
strides across the dark land spread out panorama-like
under that high ledge where the two women stood. He
was nearing in great distance-devouring steps, and it
seemed to Jirel that he diminished in stature as the space
between them lessened. Now the tree-tops were cream-
ing like black surf about his thighs. She saw anger on
his face, and she heard a little gasp behind her. She
whirled in quick terror, for surely now the witch would
slay her with no more delay, before Pav could come
near enough to prevent.

But when she turned she saw that the pale corpse-
creature had forgotten her in the frantic effort to save

herself. And she was working a magic that for an instant wiped out from Jirel's wondering mind even her own peril, even the miraculous oncoming of Pav. She had poised on her toes, and now in a swirl of shroud-like robes and snaky hair she began to spin. At first she revolved laboriously, but in a few moments the jerky whirling began to smooth out and quicken and she was revolving without effort, as if she utilized a force outside Jirel's understanding, as if some invisible whirlwind spun her faster and faster in its vortex, until she was a blur of shining, unshadowed whiteness wrapped in the dark snakes of her hair—until she was nothing but a pale mist against the forest darkness—until she had vanished utterly.

Then, as Jirel stared in dumb bewilderment, a little chill wind that somehow seemed to blow from immeasurably far distances, from cool, hollow, underground places, brushed her cheek briefly, without ruffling a single red curl. It was not a tangible wind. And from empty air a hand that was bone-hard dealt her a stinging blow in the face. An incredibly tiny, thin, far-away voice sang in her ear as if over gulfs of measurable vastness:

"That for watching my spell, red woman! And if you do not keep our bargain, you shall feel the weight of my magic. Remember!"

Then in a great gush of wind and a trample of booted feet Pav was on the ledge beside her, and no more than life-size now, tall, black, magnificent as before, radiant with arrogance and power. He stared hotly, with fathomless blackness in his eyes, at the place where the mist that was the witch had faded. Then he laughed contemptuously.

"She is safe enough—there," he said. "Let her stay. You should not have come here, Jirel of Joiry."

"I didn't come," she said in sudden, childish indignation against everything that had so mystified her, against his insolent voice and the arrogance and power of him, against the necessity for owing to him her rescue from the witch's magic. "I didn't come. The—the mountain came! All I did was look at it, and suddenly it was here."

His deep bull-bellow of laughter brought the blood angrily to her cheeks.

"You must learn that secret of your land of Romne," he said indulgently. "It is not constructed on the lines of your old world. And only by slow degrees, as you grow stronger in the magic which I shall teach you, can you learn the full measure of Romne's strangeness. It is enough for you to know now that distances here are measured in different terms from those you know. Space and matter are subordinated to the power of the mind, so that when you desire to reach a place you need only concentrate upon it to bring it into focus about you, succeeding the old landscape in which you stood.

"Later you must see Romne in its true reality, walk through Romne as Romne really is. Later, when you are my queen."

The old hot anger choked up in Jirel's throat. She was not so afraid of him now, for a weapon was in her hands which even he did not suspect. She knew his vulnerability. She cried defiantly:

"Never, then! I'd kill you first."

His scornful laughter broke into her threat.

"You could not do that," he told her, deep-voiced.

"I have said before that there is no way. Do you think I could be mistaken about that?"

She glared at him with hot, yellow eyes, indiscretion hovering on her lips. Almost she blurted it out, but not quite. In a choke of anger she turned her face away, going prickly and hot at the deep laughter behind her.

"Have you had your fill of seeking weapons against me?" he went on, still in that voice of mingling condescension and arrogance.

She hesitated a moment. Somehow she must get them both back into the hall of the image. In a voice that trembled she said at last:

"Yes."

"Shall we go back then, to my palace, and prepare for the ceremony which will make you queen?"

The deep voice was still shuddering along her nerves as the mountain behind them and the great dark world below melted together in a mirage through which, as through a veil, a flame began to glow; the flame about an image's head—an image gigantic in a great black hall whose unroofed walls closed round them in a magical swiftness. Jirel stared, realizing bewilderedly that without stirring a step she had somehow come again into the black hall where she had first opened her eyes.

A qualm of remembrance came over her as she recalled how fervently she had sworn to herself to die somehow, rather than return here into Pav's power. But now she was armed. She need have no fear now. She looked about her.

Black and enormous, the great image loomed up above them both. She lifted a gaze of new respect to that leaping diadem of flame which crowned the face that was Pav's. She did not understand what it was she must do now, or clearly how to do it, but the resolve was hot in her to take any way out that might lie open rather than submit to the dark power that dwelt in the big, black man at her side.

Hands fell upon her shoulders then, heavily. She whirled in a swirl of velvet skirts into Pav's arms, tight against his broad breast. His breath was hot in her face, and upon her like the beating of savage suns burned the intolerable blackness of his eyes. She could no more meet their heat than she could have stared into a sun. A sob of pure rage choked up in her throat as she thrust hard with both hands against the broad black chest to which she was crushed. He loosed her without a struggle. She staggered with the suddenness of it, and then he had seized her wrist in an iron grip, twisting savagely. Jirel gasped in a wrench of pain and dropped helplessly to one knee. Above her the heavy and ominous voice of Romne's king said in its deepest, most velvety burr, so that she shook to the very depths in that drum-beat of savage power.

"Resist me again and—things can happen here too dreadful for your brain to grasp even if I told you. Beware of me, Jirel, for Pav's anger is a terrible thing. You have found no weapon to conquer me, and now you must submit to the bargain you yourself proposed. Are you ready, Jirel of Joiry?"

She bent her head so that her face was hidden, and her mouth curved into a twist of fiercely smiling anticipation.

"Yes," she said softly.

Then abruptly, amazingly, upon her face a cold wind

blew, heavy with the odor of chill hollowness underground, and in her ears was the thin and tiny coldness of a voice she knew, echoing from reverberant vaults over gulfs unthinkable:

"Ask him to clothe you in bridal dress. Ask him! Ask him now!"

Across the screen of her memory flashed a face like a white-fleshed skull to whose eye-sockets cobwebby shadows clung, whose pale mouth curled in a smile of bitter scorn, maliciously urging her on. But she dared not disobey, for she had staked everything now on the accomplishment of the witch's bargain. Dangerous it might be, but there was worse danger waiting here and now, in Pav's space-black eyes. The thin shrill ceased and the tomb-smelling wind faded, and she heard her own voice saying:

"Let me up, then. Let me up—I am ready. Only am I to have no bridal dress for my wedding? For black ill becomes a bride."

He could not have heard that thin, far-calling echo of a voice, for his dark face did not change and there was no suspicion in his eyes. The iron clutch of his fingers loosened. Jirel swung to her feet lithely and faced him with downcast eyes, not daring to unveil the yellow triumph that blazed behind her lashes.

"My wedding gown," she reminded him, still in that voice of strangled gentleness.

He laughed, and his eyes sought in empty air. It was the most imperiously regal thing conceivable, that assured glance into emptiness for what, by sheer knowledge of his own power, must materialize in answer to the king of Romne's questing. And all about her, glowing into existence under the sun-hot blackness of Pav's eyes, the soft blue flames were suddenly licking.

Weakness crawled over her as the blueness seethed about her body, brushing, caressing, light as fire-tongues upon her, murmurous with the soft flickering sounds of quiet flame. A weariness like death was settling into her very bones, as if life itself were drain-ing away into the caressing ministrations of those blue and heatless flames. She exulted in her very weakness, knowing how much of her strength must be incarnate, then, in the flames which were to quench Pav's flame. And they would need strength—all she had.

Then again the cold wind blew from hollow tombs, as if through an opened door, and upon the intangible breath of it that did not stir one red curl upon her cheek, though she felt its keenness clearly, the thin, small echo of the corpse-witch's voice cried, tiny and far over spaces beyond measurement.

"Focus them on the Flame—now, now! Quickly! Ah—fool!"

And the ghost of a thin, cool laugh, stinging with scorn, drifting through the measureless voids. Reeling with weakness, Jirel obeyed. The derision in that tiny, far-away voice was like a spur to drive her, though ready anger surged up in her throat against that strange scorn for which she could find no reason. As strongly as before she felt the breath of danger when the corpse-witch spoke, but she ignored it now, knowing in her heart that Pav must die if she were ever to know peace again, let his dying cost her what it might.

She set her teeth in her red underlip and in the pain of it drove all her strength into a strong focusing upon the flame that burned around the great imaged Pav's head. What would happen she did not know, but in the fog of her weakness, stabbed by her bitten lip's pain, she fought with all the force she had to drive those flames curling like caresses about her body straight toward the flame-crown on the image's majestic brow.

And presently, in little tentative thrusts, the blue tongues that licked her so softly began to turn away from the velvety curves of her own body and reach out toward the image. Sick with weakness as the strength drained out of her into the pulling flames, she fought on, and in an arc that lengthened and stretched away the flames began to forsake her and reach flickeringly out toward the great black statue that loomed overhead.

From far away she heard Pav's deep voice shouting on a note of sudden panic:

"Jirel, Jirel! Don't! Oh, little fool, don't do it!"

It seemed to her that his voice was not that of a man afraid for his own life, but rather as if it was peril to herself he would avert. But she could pay him no heed at all now. Nothing was real but the sharp necessity to quench the image's flame, and she poured all the strength that was left to her into the rainbow of flickering blueness that was arching up toward the image.

"Jirel, Jirel!" the deep voice of Pav was storming from somewhere in the fog of her weakness. "Stop! You don't know—"

A blast of cold wind drowned the rest of his words, and:

"S-s-s! Go on!" hissed the corpse-witch's voice tinily in her ear. "Don't listen to him! Don't let him stop you! He can't touch you while the blue flames burn! Go on! Go on!"

And she went on. Half fainting, wholly blind now to everything but that stretching arc of blue, she fought.

And it lengthened as she poured more and more of her strength into it, reached up and out and grew by leaping degrees until the blue flames were mingling with the red, and over that blazing crown a dimness began to fall. From somewhere in the blind mist of her exhaustion Pav's voice shouted with a note of despair in its shudderingly vibrant depths:

"Oh, Jirel, Jirel! What have you done?"

Exultation surged up in her. The hot reserves of her anger against him flooded over and strength like wine boiled up through her body. In one tremendous burst of fierce energy she hurled every ounce of her newly-won power against the flame. Triumphantly she saw it flicker. There was a moment of guttering twilight; then abruptly the light went out and red flame and blue vanished in a breath. A crashing darkness like the weight of falling skies dropped thunderously about her.

Sick to the very soul with reactionary weakness as the tremendous effort relaxed at last, she heard from reeling distances Pav's voice call wordlessly. All about her the dark was heavy, with a crushing weight that somehow made her whole body ache as if with the pressure of deep seas. In the heaviness of it she scarcely realized that the voice was shouting at all; but even through the dimness of her failing senses she knew that there was something tremendously wrong with it. In a mighty effort she rallied herself, listening.

Yes—he was trying to speak, trying to tell her something that she knew intuitively was of infinite importance. But his voice was ceasing to be a human voice, becoming less and less articulate and more and more a mighty roaring like the voice of incalculable power. In such a voice a typhoon might speak, or a dynamo more tremendous than any man ever made.

"Jirel—Jirel—why did you . . ." So much she made out before the words rushed together and melted into that thunderous roar which was the very voice of infinity itself. The darkness was full of it—one with it—intolerable violence upon her ears, intolerable pressure of the black dark upon her body.

Through the roaring void a keen wind blew hollow with the smell of tombs. Jirel, trying to whirl to face it, found herself incapable of motion, a finite and agonized thing in the midst of crashing black thunder whose sound was torment in her brain, whose weight was crushing her very atoms in upon themselves until consciousness flickered within her like a guttering candle flame.

But there was no need to turn. Directions had ceased to be. The wind smote her turned cheek, but before her, as if through an opened door from which coldness streamed, she was aware of a white-shrouded figure floating upon the blackness; an unshadowed figure, staringly white, not touched by anything the blackness could muster against it. Even through the terrible roaring of pure power the corpse-witch's voice struck low and cool in its echo from reverberant caverns; even through the blinding dark her skull-face gleamed, the cob-webbed eyes lurid in the depths of their clinging shadows with a light that glowed from deep within the leprosy-white skull. The witch was laughing.

"O fool!" she lilted in a hollow ripple of scorn as cool as caverns underground. "Poor, presumptuous fool! Did you really think to bargain with us of the outer worlds? Did you really believe that Pav—*Pav!*—could die? No—in your little human brain how could you have known that all the Romne you saw was illusion, that Pav's human body was no real thing? Blind, hot, earthly woman, with your little hates and vengeances, how could you have reigned queen over a Romne that is Darkness itself—as you see it now? For this roaring night which engulfs you, without dimensions, without form, lightless, inchoate—this is Romne! And Romne is Pav. The land that you walked through, the mountains and plains you saw—all these were no less Pav than the human body he assumed. Nor was his height and black-bearded arrogance any more Pav himself than were the rocks and trees and black waters of Romne. Pav is Romne, and Romne is Pav—one terrible whole out of which all you saw was wrought.

"Yes, shudder, and presently, when I am through with you—die. For no human thing could live in the Romne that is real. When in your foolish vengeance you quenched the flame that burned on the image's head, you sealed your own doom. Only in the power of that flame could the illusion of the land of Romne hold itself steady about you. Only that flame in its tangible light held Romne and Pav in the semblance of reality to you, or kept the weight of the Dark from crushing your puny soul in the soft white flesh you call a body. Only the sound of my voice does it now. When I cease to speak, when the breath of my tomb-breeze ceases to blow around you—then you die."

The cool voice broke into soft and scornful laughter while darkness reeled about Jirel and the roaring was a tumult unbearable in her very brain. Was it indeed the voice of what had been Pav? Then the low, chill voice echoed on:

"But before you die I would have you look upon what you sought to slay. I would have you *see* the Darkness that is Pav and Romne, clearly and visibly, so that you might understand what manner of lover I had. And you thought to rival me! Do you think, in your pride of human endurance, you could so much as gaze for one instant upon the inferno that is—Pav!''

In that one ringing word the chill wind ceased, the voice echoed into silence from its heights of scorn, and in the darkness, black upon the black, with no sense that human flesh possesses—neither sight nor hearing nor touch—yet with hideous clarity, she saw.

She saw the Darkness. It was tremendous beyond the power of any human perceptions to endure save in the brief flash she had of it. A thunderous Darkness whose roar was vaster than anything like mere sound. The inferno of it was too hot to bear. The human Pav's eyes had blazed like black suns, intolerably, but that had been only a reflection of this infinite might. This Darkness was the incarnate blaze, and all her consciousness reeled and was in agony before it.

She thought she could not endure to look—even to exist so near to that terrible heat of darkness, but no closing of eyes could shut it out. In the fleeting instant while she saw—through closed eyes and numbed senses, conscious in every fiber of the blaze so close—a vibration from the great Thing that was beyond shape and size and matter shivered through her in a scorch of heat too hot to touch her flesh, though her soul shuddered fainting away. It was not anything like a voice, but there was intelligence in it. And in her brain she received dimly what it said.

"Sorry—would have had you—could have loved you—but go now—go instantly, before you die. . . ."

And somehow, in a way that left her mind blank with the tremendous power of it, that infinite force was commanding obedience even out of the stunning Dark. For the Darkness was Romne, and Romne was Pav, and the command ran like a shudder of dark lightning from edge to edge, expelling her from its heart in an explosion of black inferno.

Instantly, blindingly, in the numb shock of that thunderous power, the darkness ceased to engulf her. Light in a dazzle that stunned her very brain burst all around. She was spun by forces so mighty that their very tremendousness saved her from destruction, as an insect might pass unharmed through a tornado. Infinity was a whirlpool around her, and—

Flagstones pressed cool and smooth against her bare feet. She blinked dizzily. Joiry's chapel walls were rising grayly about her, familiar and dun in the dim light of dawn. She stood here in her doeskin tunic upon the flagstones and breathed in deep gusts, staring about her with dazed eyes that dwelt like lingering caresses upon the familiar things of home.

Hellsgarde

Jirel of Joiry drew rein at the edge of the hill and sat awhile in silence, looking out and down. So this was Hellsgarde. She had seen it many times in her mind's eye as she saw it now from the high hill in the yellow light of sunset that turned every pool of the marshes to shining glass. The long causeway to the castle stretched out narrowly between swamps and reeds up to the gate of that grim and eery fortress set alone among the quicksands. This same castle in the marshes, seen at evening from the high hilltop, had haunted her dreams for many nights now.

"You'll find it by sunset only, my lady," Guy of Garlot had told her with a sidelong grin marring his comely dark face. "Mists and wilderness ring it round, and there's magic in the swamps about Hellsgarde. Magic—and worse, if legends speak truth. You'll never come upon it save at evening."

Sitting her horse now on the hilltop, she remembered the grin in his black eyes and cursed him in a whisper. There was such a silence over the whole evening world that by instinct she dared not speak aloud. Dared not? It was no normal silence. Bird-song did not break it, and no leaves rustled. She huddled her shoulders together a little under the tunic of link-mail she wore and prodded her horse forward down the hill.

Guy of Garlot—Guy of Garlot! The hoofbeats thumped out the refrain all the way downhill. Black Guy with his thinly smiling lips and his slanted dark eyes and his unnatural comeliness—unnatural because Guy, within, was ugly as sin itself. It seemed no design of the good God that such sinfulness should wear Guy's dark beauty for a fleshly garment.

The horse hesitated at the head of the causeway which stretched between the marsh pools toward Hellsgarde. Jirel shook the reins impatiently and smiled a one-sided smile downward at his twitching ears.

"I go as loath as you," she told him. "I go wincing under spurs too, my pretty. But go I must, and you too." And she cursed Guy again in a lingering whisper as the slow hoofbeats reverberated upon the stone arches of the causeway.

Beyond it loomed Hellsgarde, tall and dark against the sunset. All around her lay the yellow light of evening, above her in the sky, below her in the marshy pools beneath which quicksands quivered. She wondered who last had ridden this deserted causeway in the yellow glow of sunset, under what dreadful compulsion.

For no one sought Hellsgarde for pleasure. It was Guy of Garlot's slanting grin that drove Jirel across the marshes this evening—Guy and the knowledge that a score of her best men-at-arms lay shivering tonight in his dripping dungeons with no hope of life save the hope that she might buy their safety. And no riches could tempt Black Guy, not even Jirel's smoothly curving beauty and the promise of her full-lipped smile. And Garlot Castle, high on its rocky mountain peak, was impregnable against even Jirel's masterfully planned attacks. Only one thing could tempt the dark lord of Garlot, and that a thing without a name.

"It lies in Hellsgarde, my lady," he had told her with that hateful smooth civility which his sleek grin so belied. "And it is indeed Hell-guarded. Andred of Hellsgarde died defending it two hundred years ago, and I have coveted it all my life. But I love living, my lady! I would not venture into Hellsgarde for all the wealth in Christendom. If you want your men back alive, bring me the treasure that Andred died to save."

"But what is it, coward?"

Guy had shrugged. "Who knows? Whence it came and what it was no man can say now. You know the tale as well as I, my lady. He carried it in a leather casket locked with an iron key. It must have been small—but very precious. Precious enough to die for, in the end—as I do not propose to die, my lady! You fetch it to me and buy twenty lives in the bargain."

She had sworn at him for a coward, but in the end she had gone. For after all, she was Joiry. Her man were hers to bully and threaten and command, but they were hers to die for too, if need be. She was afraid, but she remembered her men in Garlot's dungeons with the rack and the boot awaiting them, and she rode on.

The causeway was so long. Sunset had begun to tarnish a little in the bright pools of the marsh, and she could look up at the castle now without being blinded by the dazzle beyond. A mist had begun to rise in level layers from the water, and the smell of it was not good in her nostrils.

Hellsgarde—Hellsgarde and Andred. She did not want to remember the hideous old story, but she could not keep her mind off it this evening. Andred had been a big, violent man, passionate and wilful and very cruel. Men hated him, but when the tale of his dying spread abroad even his enemies pitied Andred of Hellsgarde.

For the rumor of his treasure had drawn at last besiegers whom he could not overcome. Hellsgarde gate had fallen and the robber nobles who captured the castle searched in vain for the precious casket which Andred guarded. Torture could not loosen his lips, though they tried very terribly to make him speak. He was a powerful man, stubborn and brave. He lived a long while under torment, but he would not betray the hiding-place of his treasure.

They tore him limb from limb at last and cast his dismembered body into the quicksands, and came away empty-handed. No one ever found Andred's treasure.

Since then for two hundred years Hellsgarde had lain empty. It was a dismal place, full of mists and fevers from the marsh, and Andred did not lie easy in the quicksands where his murderers had cast him. Dismembered and scattered broadcast over the marshes, .yet he would not lie quiet. He had treasured his mysterious wealth with a love stronger than death itself, and legend said he walked Hellsgarde as jealously in death as in life.

In the two hundred years searchers had gone fearfully to ransack the empty halls of Hellsgarde for that casket—gone and vanished. There was magic in the marshes, and a man could come upon the castle only by sunset, and after sunset Andred's violent ghost rose out of the quicksands to guard the thing he died for. For generations now no one had been so foolhardy as to venture upon the way Jirel rode tonight.

She was drawing near the gateway. There was a broad platform before it, just beyond the place where Andred's drawbridge had once barred the approach to Hellsgarde. Long ago the gap in the causeway had been filled in with rubble by searchers who would reach the castle on horseback, and Jirel had thought of passing the night upon that platform under the gate arch, so that dawn might find her ready to begin her search.

But—the mists between her and the castle had thickened, and her eyes might be playing her false—but were not those the shapes of men drawn up in a double row before the doorway of Hellsgarde? Hellsgarde, that had stood empty and haunted these two hundred years? Blinking through the dazzle of sun on water and the thickening of the mists, she rode on toward the gateway. She could feel the horse trembling between her knees, and with every step he grew more and more reluctant to go on. She set her teeth and forced him ahead resolutely, swallowing her own terror.

They *were* the figures of men, two rows of them, waiting motionless before the gate. But even through the mist and the sun-dazzle she could see that something was wrong. They were so still—so unearthly still as they faced her. And the horse was shying and trembling until she could scarcely force him forward.

She was quite near before she saw what was wrong, though she knew that at every forward step the obscure frightfulness about these guardsmen grew greater. But she was almost upon them before she realized why. They were all dead.

The captain at their front stood slumped down upon the great spear that propped him on his feet, driven through his throat so that the point stood out above his neck as he sagged there, his head dragging forward until his cheek lay against the shaft which transfixed him.

And so stood all the rest, behind him in a double row, reeling drunkenly upon the spears driven through throat or chest or shoulder to prop them on their feet in the hideous semblance of life.

So the company of dead men kept guard before the gateway of Hellsgarde. It was not unfitting—dead men guarding a dead castle in the barren deadlands of the swamp.

Jirel sat her horse before them for a long moment in silence, feeling the sweat gather on her forehead, clenching her hands on the pommel of the saddle. So far as she knew, no other living person in decades had ridden the long causeway to Hellsgarde; certainly no living man had dwelt in these haunted towers in generations. Yet—here stood the dead men reeling against the spears which had slain them but would not let them fall. Why?—how?—when? . . .

Death was no new thing to Jirel. She had slain too many men herself to fear it. But the ghastly unexpectedness of this dead guard! It was one thing to steel oneself to enter an empty ruin, quite another to face a double row of standing dead men whose blood still ran in dark rivulets, wetly across the stones at their feet. Still wet—they had died today, then. Today while she struggled cursing through the wilderness something had slain them here, something had made a jest of death as it propped them on their dead feet with their dead faces toward the causeway along which she must come riding. Had that something expected her? Could the dead Andred have known—?

She caught herself with a little shudder and shrugged beneath the mail, clenching her fingers on the pommel, swallowing hard. (Remember your men—remember Guy of Garlot—remember that you are Joiry!) The memory of Guy's comely face, bright with mockery, put steel into her and she snapped her chin up with a murmured oath. These men were dead—they could not hinder her. . . .

Was that motion among the ghastly guard? Her heart leaped to her throat and she gripped the saddle between nervous knees with a reflex action that made the horse shudder. For one of the men in the row before her was slipping silently toward the flagstones. Had the spear-butt slid on the bloody tiles? Had a breeze dislodged his precarious balance? There was no breeze. But with a curious little sigh from collapsing lungs he folded gently downward to his knees, to his side, to a flattened proneness on the stones. And a dark stream of blood trickled from his mouth to snake across the pavement as he lay there.

Jirel sat frozen. It was a nightmare. Only in nightmares could such things happen. This unbearable silence in the dying sunset, no breeze, no motion, no sound. Not even a ripple upon the mirroring waters lying so widely around her below the causeway, light draining from their surfaces. Sky and water were paling as if all life receded from about her, leaving only Jirel on her trembling horse facing the dead men and the dead castle. She scarcely dared move lest the thump of her mount's feet on the stones dislodge the balance of another man. And she thought she could not bear to see motion again among those motionless ranks. She could not bear it, and yet—and yet if something did not break the spell soon the screams gathering in her throat would burst past her lips and she knew she would never stop screaming.

A harsh scraping sounded beyond the dead guardsmen. Her heart squeezed itself to a stop. And then the blood began to thunder through her veins and her heart leaped and fell and leaped again in a frenzied pounding against the mail of her tunic.

For beyond the men the great door of Hellsgarde was swinging open. She gripped her knees against the saddle until her thighs ached, and her knuckles were bone-white upon the pommel. She made no move toward the great sword at her side. What use is a sword against dead men?

But it was no dead man who looked out under the arch of the doorway, stooped beneath his purple tunic with the heartening glow of firelight from beyond reddening his bowed shoulders. There was something odd about his pale, pinched face upturned to hers across the double line of dead defenders between them. After a moment she recognized what it was—he had the face of a hunchback, but there was no deformity upon his shoulders. He stooped a little as if with weariness, but he carried no hump. Yet it was the face of a cripple if she had ever seen one. His back was straight, but could his soul be? Would the good God have put the sign of deformity upon a human creature without cause? But he was human—he was real. Jirel sighed from the bottom of her lungs.

"Good evening to you, my lady," said the hunchback (but he was not humped) in a flat, ingratiating voice.

"*These*—did not find it good," said Jirel shortly, gesturing. And the man grinned.

"My master's jest," he said.

Jirel looked back to the rows of standing dead, her heart quieting a little. Yes, a man might find a grim sort of humor in setting such a guard before his door. If a living man had done it, for an understanding reason, then the terror of the unknown was gone. But the man—

"Your master?" she echoed.

"My lord Alaric of Hellsgarde—you did not know?"

"Know what?" demanded Jirel flatly. She was beginning to dislike the fellow's sidelong unctuousness.

"Why, that my lord's family has taken residence here after many generations away."

"Sir Alaric is of Andred's kin?"

"He is."

Jirel shrugged mentally. It was God's blessing to feel the weight of terror lift from her, but this would complicate matters. She had not known that Andred left descendants, though it might well be so. And if they lived here, then be sure they would already have ransacked the castle from keep to dungeon for that nameless treasure which Andred had died to save and had not yet forsaken, were rumor true. Had they found it? There was only one way to learn that.

"I am nighted in the marshes," she said as courteously as she could manage. "Will your master give me shelter until morning?"

The hunchback's eyes—(but he was no hunchback, she must stop thinking of him so!)—his eyes slid very quickly, yet very comprehensively, from her tanned and red-lipped face downward over the lifting curves of her under the molding chainmail, over her bare brown knees and slim, steel-greaved legs. There was a deeper unctuousness in his voice as he said:

"My master will make you very welcome, lady. Ride in."

Jirel kicked her horse's flank and guided him, snorting and trembling, through the gap in the ranks of dead men which the falling soldier had left. He was a battle-charger, he was used to dead men; yet he shuddered as he minced through these lines.

The courtyard within was warm with the light of the great fire in its center. Around it a cluster of loutish men in leather jerkins looked up as she passed.

"Wat, Piers—up, men!" snapped the man with the hunchback's face. "Take my lady's horse."

Jirel hesitated a moment before she swung from the saddle, her eyes dubious upon the faces around her. She thought she had never seen such brutish men before, and she wondered at the lord who dared employ them. Her own followers were tough enough, reckless, hard fellows without fear or scruple. But at least they were men. These louts around the fire seemed scarcely more than beasts; let greed or anger stir them and no man alive could control their wildness. She wondered with what threats of punishment the lord Alaric held sway here, what sort of man he must be to draw his guard from the very dregs of humanity.

The two who took her horse stared at her under shaggy beetle-brows. She flashed them a poison glance as she turned to follow the purple cloak of her guide. Her eyes were busy. Hellsgarde had been a strong fortress in Andred's day; under Alaric it was well manned, but she thought she sensed a queer, hovering sullenness in the very air as she followed her guide across the courtyard, down a passageway, under an arch into the great hall.

The shadows of two hundred haunted years hovered under the lofty roof-beams. It was cold here, damp with the breath of the swamps outside, dark with two centuries of ugly legend and the terrible tradition of murder. But Alaric before the fire in his scarlet tunic seemed pleasantly at home. The great blaze roaring up the chimney from six-foot logs drove back the chill and the dark and the damp a little in a semicircle about the fireplace, and in that semicircle a little company of brightly clad people sat silent, watching Jirel and her guide cross the echoing flags of the great hall toward them.

It was a pleasant scene, warm and firelit and bright with color, but even at a distance, something was wrong—something in the posture of the people crouching before the blaze, something in their faces. Jirel knew a moment of wild wonder if all this were real. Did she really walk a haunted ruin empty two hundred years? Were the people flesh and blood, or only the bright shadows of her own imagination that had so desperately longed for companionship in the haunted marsh?

But no, there was nothing illusive about Alaric in his

high-backed chair, his face a pale oval watching her
progress. A humped dwarf leaned above his shoulder,
fingers suspended over his lute-strings as he stared. On
cushions and low benches by the fire a handful of
women and girls, two young boys in bright blue, a pair
of greyhounds with the firelight scarlet in their eyes—
these made up the rest of the company.

Jirel's narrow yellow gaze summed them up as she
crossed the hall. Striding smoothly in her thigh-length
hauberk, she knew she was a figure on which a man's
eyes must linger. Her supple height, the pleasant
smooth curves of her under mail, the long, shapely legs
bare beneath the linked metal of her hauberk, the swinging of the long sword whose weight upon its belt pulled
in her waist to tigerish slimness—Alaric's eyes missed
nothing of all these. Deliberately she tossed the dark
cloak back over her shoulders, letting the firelight take
the sleek mailed curves of her in a bright glimmer, flash
from the shining greaves that clasped her calves. It was
not her way to postpone the inevitable. Let Alaric learn
in his first long stare how splendid a creature was
Joiry's lady. And as for those women at his feet—well,
let them know too.

She swaggered to a halt before Alaric, resting a hand
on her sword-hilt, tossing back the cloak that had
swirled about her as she swung to a stop. His face, half
in the shadow of the chair, tilted up to her leanly. Here
was no burly brute of a man such as she had half
expected on the evidence of the men-at-arms he kept.
He was of middle years, his face deeply grooved with
living, his nose a hawk-beak, his mouth a sword-gash.

And there was something oddly wrong with his features, a queer cast upon them that made him seem akin

to the purple-clad courtier hovering at Jirel's elbow, to the grinning jester who peered across the chair-back. With a little twist of the heart she saw what it was. There was no physical likeness between master and men in any feature, but the shadow of deformity lay upon all three faces, though only the hunchback wore it honestly. Looking at those faces, one would have sworn that each of the trio went limping through life under the burden of a crooked spine. Perhaps, Jirel thought involuntarily, with a small shudder, the master and the courtier as well as the fool did indeed carry a burden, and if they did she thought she would prefer the jester's to theirs. His at least was honest and of the flesh. But theirs must be of the spirit, for surely, she thought again, God in His wisdom does not for nothing mark a whole and healthy man with a cripple's face. It was a deformity of the soul that looked out of the eyes meeting hers.

And because the thought frightened her she swung her shoulders until the cape swirled wide, and flashed her white teeth in a smile more boldly reckless than the girl behind it felt.

"You must not crave the company of strangers, sir—you keep a discouraging guard before your gate!"

Alaric did not smile. "Honest travelers are welcome here," he said very smoothly. "But the next robbers who ride our causeway will think twice before they storm the gates. We have no gallows here where thieves may swing in chains, but I think the guard before my castle will be warning enough to the next raiders who come."

"A grisly sort of warning," said Jirel. And then, with belated courtesy, "I am Jirel of Joiry. I missed my way in the marsh tonight—I shall be grateful for your hospitality.''

"And we for your presence, Lady Jirel."

Alaric's voice was oily, but his eyes raked her openly. She felt other eyes upon her back too, and her red hair stiffened a little at the roots with a prickling uneasiness. "We keep a small court here at Hellsgarde," went on Alaric's voice. "Damara, Ettard, Isoud, Morgaine—all of you, make our guest welcome!"

Jirel swung round with a swirl of her long cloak to face the women, wondering at the subtle slight to their dignity, for Alaric made no effort to introduce them separately.

She thought they crouched a little on their low seats by the fire, looking up with the queer effect of women peering fearfully from under lowered brows, though she could not have said why they seemed so, for they met her eyes squarely. And upon these faces too lay that strange shadow of deformity, not so definitely as upon the men's, but visible in the firelight. All of them were thin creatures with big eyes showing a rather shocking space of whiteness around the staring irises. Their cheek-bones were sharp in the firelight, so that shadows stood hollowly beneath.

The woman who had risen when Alaric said "Damara" was as tall as Jirel, strongly made under her close green gown, but her face too had that queer hollow look and her eyes stared too whitely under wide-open lids. She said in a tight voice:

"Sit down by the fire and warm yourself, lady. We dine in a few minutes."

Jirel sank to the low cushioned stool she dragged

forward, one leg doubled under her for instant rising, her sword-hilt and sword-hand free. There was something wrong here. She could feel it in the air.

The two dogs growled a little and shifted away from her on the floor, and even that was—wrong. Dogs had fawned on her always—until now. And the firelight was so red in their eyes. . . .

Looking away uneasily from those unnaturally red eyes, she saw the boys' features clearly for the first time, and her heart contracted a little. For naked evil was upon these two young faces. The others wore their shadow of deformity elusively, a thing more sensed than seen. It might be only a trick of her legend-fed imagination that put evil there. But the two young lads had the faces of devils, long faces with high cheekbones and slitted, lusterless eyes. Jirel shuddered a little inwardly. What sort of company had she stumbled into, where the very children and dogs wore evil like a garment?

She drew a deep breath and glanced around the circle of still faces that watched her wordlessly, with an intentness like that of—of beasts of prey? Her pride rebelled at that. Joiry was ever the predator, not the prey! She squared her cleft chin and said with determined casualness:

"You have dwelt here long?"

She could have sworn a look went round the semicircle before the fire, a swift, amused glance from face to face as if they shared a secret. Yet not an eye wavered from hers. Only the two boys leaned together a little, and the look of evil brightened upon their wicked young faces. Alaric answered after the briefest possible pause:

"Not long. Nor will we stay long—now." There

was a subtle menace in it, though Jirel could not have said why. And again that feeling of knowledge shared ran like a strong current around the circle, a little quiver as if a dreadful amusement were almost stirring in the air. But not a face changed or turned. The eyes were still eager—almost avid—upon the bright, strong face of Jirel with the firelight warming her golden tan and touching her red curls to flame and trembling upon the soft curve of her under-lip. For all the bright clothes of the company around her, she had the sudden feeling that dark robes and dark eyes and dark faces hemmed her in—like shadows around a fire.

The conversation had come to a full stop; the eyes never wavered from her. She could not fathom this strange interest, for it was queer Alaric had not asked anything at all about her coming. A woman alone in this wilderness at night was sufficiently unusual to arouse interest, yet no one seemed concerned to ask how she had come there. Why, then, this concerted, deep interest in the sight of her?

To conquer the little tremor she could not quite ignore she said boldly:

"Hellsgarde of the Marshes has an ugly reputation, my lord. I wonder you dare dwell here—or do you know the old tale?"

Unmistakably this time that quiver of amusement flashed around the circle, though not an eye left hers. Alaric's voice was dry as he answered:

"Yes—yes, we know the tale. We are—not afraid."

And suddenly Jirel was quite sure of a strange thing. Something in his voice and his words told her very surely that they had not come in spite of the terrible old legend, but *because of it*.

No normal people would deliberately seek out a haunted and blood-stained ruin for a dwelling-place, yet there could be no mistaking the implication in Alaric's voice, in the unspoken mirth at her words that ran like a whisper around the circle. She remembered those dead men at the door. What normal person could make a joke so grisly? No, no—this company was as definitely abnormal as a company of monsters. One could not sit with them long even in silence without sensing that. The look of abnormality upon their faces did not lie—it was a sure sign of a deformity of the soul.

The conversation had stopped again. To break the nerve-racking silence Jirel said:

"We hear many strange tales of Hellsgarde"—and knew she was talking too much, but could not stop—anything was better than that staring silence—"tales of treasure and—and—is it true that one can come upon Hellsgarde Castle only in the sunset—as I did?"

Alaric paused deliberately for a moment before he answered with as deliberate evasiveness. "There are stranger tales than that of Hellsgarde—and who can say how much of truth is in them? Treasure? There may well be treasure here. Many have come seeking it—and remained, for ever."

Jirel remembered the dead men at the door, and she shot Alaric a yellow glare that would have clanged like the meeting of blades with his stare—had he met it. He was looking up into the shadows of the ceiling, and he was smiling a little. Did he suspect her errand? He had asked no questions . . . Jirel remembered Guy of Garlot's smile as he sent her on this quest, and a murderous wonder began to take shape in her mind. If Guy had known—if he had deliberately sent her into this peril—she let herself sink for a moment into a luxury of picturing that comely smile smashed in by the handle of her sword. . . .

They were watching her. She came back with a jerk and said at random:

"How cold the marshes are after sunset!" And she shivered a little, not until that moment realizing the chill of the great hall.

"We find it—pleasant," murmured Alaric, watching her.

The others were watching too, and again she sensed that ripple of subtle amusement running around the circle that closed her out of a secret shared. They were here for a purpose. She knew it suddenly: a strange, unfathomable purpose that bound them together with almost one mind, so that thoughts seemed to flow soundlessly from brain to brain; a purpose that included her now, and in no pleasant way. Danger was in the air, and she alone here by night in the deserted marshes, among these queer, abnormal people who watched her with an avid and unwavering eagerness. Well, she had been in peril before, and hewed her way out again.

A slovenly wench in a ragged smock tiptoed clumsily out of the shadows to murmur in Damara's ear, and Jirel felt with conscious relief the removal of at least one pair of staring eyes as the woman turned to nod. Jirel's gaze was scornful on the girl. A queer household they kept here—the bestial retainers, the sluttish wench in her soiled gown.

Not even Joiry's kitchen maids were so slovenly clad.

Damara turned back to the fire. "Shall we dine now?" she asked.

Every face around the fire brightened magically, and Jirel was conscious of a little loosening of the tension in her own mind. The very fact that the thought of food pleased them made the whole group seem more normal. And yet—she saw it in a moment—this was not even a normal eagerness. There was something a little horrid about the gleam in every eye, the avid hunger on every face. For a little while the thought of food supplanted herself in their interest, and that terrible battery of watchfulness forsook her. It was like an actual weight lifted. She breathed deeper.

Frowsy kitchen scullions and a pair of unwashed girls were carrying in the planks and trestles for the table, setting it up by the fire.

"We dine alone," Alaric was explaining as the group around the fire reshifted itself to make way. It seemed a witless sort of fastidiousness to Jirel, particularly since they let themselves be served by such shamefully unkempt lackeys. Other households dined all together, from lord to stable hands, at the long T-shaped tables where the salt divided noblesse from peasantry. But perhaps Alaric dared not allow those beast-wild men of his even that familiarity. And she was conscious of a tiny disappointment that the company of these staring, strange-faced people was not to be leavened even by the brutish earthiness of their retainers. The men-at-arms seemed scarcely human, but at least it was a normal, open sort of brutality, something she could understand.

When the table was ready Alaric seated her at his right hand, beside the two evil-faced youngsters who sat preternaturally quiet. Young lads of that age were scufflers and squirmers at table in the company she knew. It was another count of eeriness against them that they scarcely moved save to reach for food.

Who were they? she wondered. Alaric's sons? Pages or squires from some noble family? She glanced around the table in deepening bewilderment, looking for signs of kinship on the shadowed faces, finding nothing but that twist of deformity to link the company together. Alaric had made no attempt to introduce any of them, and she could not guess what relationship bound them all together in this close, unspoken communion. She met the eyes of the dwarf at Alaric's elbow and looked quickly away again, angry at his little comprehending grin. He had been watching her.

There was no conversation after the meat was brought in. The whole company fell upon it with such a starved eagerness that one might think they had not dined in weeks before now. And not even their food tasted right or normal.

It looked well enough, but there was a subtle seasoning about it that made Jirel gag and lay down her knife after the first taste—a flavor almost of decay, and a sort of burning bitterness she could not put a name to, that lingered on the tongue long after the food itself was swallowed. Everything stank of it, the roast, the bread, the few vegetables, even the bitter wine.

After a brave effort, for she was hungry, Jirel gave up and made not even the pretense of eating. She sat with her arms folded on the table edge, right hand hanging near her sword, watching the ravenous company devour their tainted food. It was no wonder, she realized suddenly, that they ate alone. Surely not even the dull palates of their retainers could accept this revoltingly seasoned meat.

Alaric sat back at last in his high-backed chair, wiping his dagger on a morsel of bread.

"You do not hunger, Lady Jirel?" he asked, tilting a brow at her still-heaped trencher. She could not help her little grimace as she glanced down.

"Not now," she said, with wry humor.

Alaric did not smile. He leaned forward to pick up upon his dagger the thick slab of roast before her, and tossed it to the hearth. The two greyhounds streaked from beneath the table to growl over it hungrily, and Alaric glanced obliquely at Jirel, with a hint of a one-sided smile, as he wiped the knife again and sheathed it.

If he meant her to understand that the dogs were included in this queer closed circle of his she caught it. Obviously there had been a message in that act and smile.

When the table had been cleared away and the last glimmer of sunset had faded from the high, narrow slits of the windows, a sullen fellow in frieze went around the hall with a long pole-torch, lighting the cressets.

"Have you visited Hellsgarde before, my lady?" inquired Alaric. And as Jirel shook her head, "Let me show you the hall then, and my forefathers' arms and shields. Who knows?—you may find quarterings of your own among our escutcheons."

Jirel shuddered at the thought of discovering even a remote kinship with Hellsgarde's dwellers, but she laid her hand reluctantly on the arm he offered and let him lead her away from the fire out under the echoing vaults of the hall where cressets brought the shadows to life.

The hall was as Andred's murderers must have left it two centuries ago. What shields and armor had not fallen from the walls were thick with rust in the damp air of the marshes, and the tatters of pennons and tapestries had long ago taken on a uniform color of decay. But Alaric seemed to savor the damp and the desolation as a normal man might savor luxury. Slowly he led her around the hall, and she could feel the eyes of the company, who had resumed their seats by the fire, follow her all the way with one unwinking stare.

The dwarf had taken up his lute again and struck occasional chords in the echoing silence of the hall, but except for that there was no sound but the fall of their feet on the rushless flagstones and the murmur of Alaric's voice pointing out the vanished glories of Hellsgarde Castle.

They paused at the side of the big room farthest from the fire, and Alaric said in an unctuous voice, his eyes seeking Jirel's with curious insistence:

"Here on this spot where we stand, lady, died Andred of Hellsgarde two hundred years ago."

Jirel looked down involuntarily. Her feet were planted on the great blotch of a spreading stain that had the rough outline of a beast with questing head and paws outsprawled. It was a broad, stain, black and splattered upon the stone. Andred must have been a big man. He had bled terribly on that day two centuries past.

Jirel felt her host's eyes on her face full of a queer anticipation, and she caught her breath a little to speak, but before she could utter a sound, quite suddenly there was a riot of wind all about them, shrieking out of nowhere in a whirlwind gust that came ravening with such fury that the cressets went out all together in one breath and darkness like a blow fell upon the hall.

In the instant of that blackness, while the whole great hall was black and vocal and·bewildering with storm-wind, as if he had been waiting avidly for this moment all evening a man's arm seized Jirel in a grip like death and a mouth came down upon hers in a more savagely violent and intimate kiss than she had ever known before. It all burst upon her so quickly that her impressions confused and ran together into one gust of terrible anger against Alaric as she struggled helplessly against that iron arm and ravenous mouth, while the storm-wind shrieked in the darkness. She was conscious of nothing but the arm, the mouth, the insolent hand. She was not pressed against a man's body, but the strength of the arm was like steel about her.

And in the same moment of the seizure the arm was dragging her violently across the floor with irresistible force, never slackening its crushing grip, the kiss in all its revolting intimacy still ravaging her muted mouth. It was as if the kiss, the crush of the arm, the violence of the hand, the howl of the wind and the drag across the room were all but manifestations of a single vortex of violence.

It could not have lasted more than seconds. She had an impression of big, square, wide-spaced teeth against her lips and the queer violence behind them manifest not primarily in the savageness of the kiss or the embrace, or the wild drag across the room, but more as if all these were mere incidents to a burning vehemence behind them that beat like heat all around her.

Choking with impotent fury, she tried to struggle, tried to scream. But there was no chest to push for leverage and no body to arch away from, and she could not resist. She could only make dumb animal sounds in her throat, sealed in behind the storming violation of that mouth.

She had scarcely time to think, it happened so quickly. She was too stunned by the violence and suddenness of the attack even to wonder at the absence of anything but the mouth, the arm, the hand. But she did have the distinct impression of walls closing in around her, as if she were being dragged out of the great open hall into a narrow closet. It was somehow as if that violence beating all about her were confined and made more violent by the presence of close walls very near.

It was all over so quickly that even as that feeling of closing walls dawned upon her she heard the little amazed cries of the others as the cressets were blown out all together. It was as if time had moved faster for her than for them. In another instant someone must have thrown brush on the fire, for the great blaze in the cavern of the chimney roared up with a gush of light and sound, for a moment beating back the darkness in the hall.

And Jirel was staggering alone in the center of the big room. No one was near her, though she could have sworn upon the cross-hilt of her sword that a split second before the heavy mouth had crushed her muted lips. It was gone now as if it had never been. Walls did not enclose her; there was no wind, there was no sound in the great hall.

Alaric stood over the black blotch of Andred's blood at the other side of the hall. She thought she must have known subconsciously after the first moment that it was not he whose lips ravaged her bruised mouth. That flaming vehemence was not in him. No, though he had been the only man near her when the dark closed down, he was not the man whose outrageous kiss still throbbed on her mouth.

She lifted an unsteady hand to those bruised lips and stared around her wildly, gasping for lost breath, half sobbing with fury.

The others were still around the fire, half the width of the room away. And as the light from the replenished blaze leaped up, she saw the blankness of their momentary surprise vanish before one leaping flame of avid hope that for an instant lit every face alike. With long running strides Alaric reached her side. In her dazed confusion she felt his hands on her arms shaking her eagerly, heard him gabbling in a tongue she did not know:

"G'hasta-est? Tai g'hasta? Tai g'hasta?"

Angrily, she shook him off as the other closed round her in an eagerly excited group, babbling all together, *"G'hasta tai? Est g'hasta?"*

Alaric recovered his poise first. In a voice shaking with the first emotion she had heard from him he demanded with almost desperate eagerness.

"What was it? What happened? Was it—was it—?" But he seemed scarcely to dare name the thing his whole soul longed for, though the tremble of hope was in his voice.

Jirel caught herself on the verge of answering. Deliberately she paused to fight down the dizzy weakness that still swam in her brain, drooping her lids to hide the calculation that came up like a flame behind her yellow eyes. For the first time she had a leverage over these mysterious people. She knew something they frantically desired to know, and she must make full use of the knowledge she scarcely knew she had.

"H-happened?" The stammer was not entirely feigned. "There was a—a wind, and darkness—I don't know—it was all over so quickly." And she glanced up into the gloom with not wholly assumed terror. Whatever that thing had been—it was no human agency. She could have sworn that the instant before the light flared up, walls were closing around her as tightly as a tomb's walls; yet they had vanished more lightly than mist in the glow of the fire. But that mouth upon hers, those big, squarely spaced teeth against her lips, the crush of the brutal arm—nothing could have been more tangible. Yet there had been only the arm, the mouth, the hand. No body. . . . With a sudden shudder that made the goose-flesh ripple along her limbs she remembered that Andred had been dismembered before they flung him into the quicksands. . . . Andred. . . .

She did not know she had said it aloud, but Alaric pounced like a cat on the one word that left her lips.

"Andred? Was it Andred?"

Jirel recovered herself with a real effort, clenching her teeth to stop their chattering.

"Andred? He died two hundred years ago!"

"He will never die until—" One of the young boys with the evil faces said that much before Alaric whirled on him angrily, yet with curious deference.

"Silence! . . . Lady Jirel, you asked me if the legends of Hellsgarde are true. Now I tell you that the tale of Andred is. We believe he still walks the halls where his treasure lies hid, and we—we—" He hesitated, and Jirel saw a strong look of calculation dawn upon his face. He went on smoothly, "We believe there is but one way to find that treasure. Only the ghost of Andred can lead us there. And Andred's ghost has been—elusive, until now."

She could have sworn that he had not meant to say just that when he began to speak. She was surer of it when she saw the little flicker of communication ripple around the circle of faces closing her in. Amusement at a subtle jest in which she did not share . . . it was on every face around her, the hollow-cheeked women's white-rimmed staring eyes brightened, the men's faces twitched a little with concealed mirth. Suddenly she felt smothered by abnormality and mystery and that subtle, perilous amusement without reason.

She was more shaken by her terrifying experience than she would have cared to admit. She had little need to feign weakness as she turned away from them toward the fire, eager to escape their terrible company even though it meant solitude in this haunted dark. She said:

"Let me—rest by the fire. Perhaps it—it—he won't return."

"But he must return!" She thought that nearly every voice around her spoke simultaneously, and eager agreement was bright upon every face. Even the two dogs had thrust themselves forward among the legs of the little crowd around Jirel, and their shadowed eyes, still faintly aglow as if with borrowed firelight, followed the conversation from face to face as if they too understood. Their gazes turned redly up to Alaric now as he said:

"For many nights we have waited in vain for the force that was Andred to make itself known to us. Not until you come does he create that vortex which—

which is necessary if we are to find the treasure.''
Again, at that word, Jirel thought she felt a little current
of amusement ripple from listener to listener. Alaric
went on in his smooth voice, ''We are fortunate to find
one who has the gift of summoning Andred's spirit to
Hellsgarde. I think there must be in you a kindred
fierceness which Andred senses and seeks. We must
call him out of the dark again—and we must use your
power to do it.''

Jirel stared around her incredulously. ''You would
call—*that*—up again?''

Eyes gleamed at her with a glow that was not of the
firelight. ''We would indeed,'' murmured the evil-
faced boy at her elbow. ''And we will not wait much
longer. . . .''

''But—God's Mercy!'' said Jirel, ''—are all the
legends wrong? They say Andred's spirit swoops down
with sudden death on all who trespass in Hellsgarde.
Why do you talk as if only I could evoke it? Do you
want to die so terribly? I do not! I won't endure *that*
again if you kill me for it. I'll have no more of Andred's
kisses!''

There was a pulse of silence around the circle for a
moment. Eyes met and looked away again. Then Alaric
said:

''Andred resents only outsiders in Hellsgarde, not
his own kinsmen and their retainers. Moreover, those
legends you speak of are old ones, telling tales of
long-ago trespassers in this castle.

''With the passage of years the spirits of the violent
dead draw farther and farther away from their death-
scenes. Andred is long dead, and he revisits Hellsgarde

Castle less often and less vindictively as the years go by. We have striven a long while to draw him back— but you alone succeeded. No, lady, you must endure Andred's violence once again, or—"

"Or what?" demanded Jirel coldly, dropping her hand to her sword.

"There is no alternative." Alaric's voice was inflexible. "We are many to your one. We will hold you here until Andred comes again."

Jirel laughed. "You think Joiry's men will let her vanish without a trace? You'll have such a storming about Hellsgarde walls as—"

"I think not, lady. What soldiers will dare follow when a braver one than any of them was vanished in Hellsgarde? No, Joiry, your men will not seek you here. You—"

Jirel's sword flamed in the firelight as she sprang backward, dragging it clear. The blade flashed once— and then arms like iron pinioned her from behind. For a dreadful moment she thought they were Andred's, and her heart turned over. But Alaric smiled, and she knew. It was the dwarf who had slipped behind her at an unspoken message from his master, and if his back was weak his arms were not. He had a bear's grip upon her and she could not wrench herself free.

Struggling, sobbing curses, kicking hard with her steel-spurred heels, she could not break his hold. There was a murmurous babble all around her of that strange, haunting tongue again, *"L'vraista! Tai g'hasta vrai! El vraist' tai lau!"* And the two devil-faced boys dived for her ankles. They clung like ghoulishly grinning apes, pinning her feet to the floor. And Alaric stepped forward to wrench the sword from her hand. He murmured something in their queer speech, and the crowd scattered purposefully.

Fighting hard, Jirel was scarcely aware of their intention before it was accomplished. But she heard the sudden splash of water on blazing logs and the tremendous hissing of steam as the fire went out and darkness fell like a blanket upon the shadowy hall. The crowd had melted away from her into the dark, and now the grip on her ankles suddenly ceased and the great arms that held her so hard heaved in a mighty swing.

Choking with fury, she reeled into the darkness. There was nothing to stop her, and those mighty arms had thrown her hard. She fell and slid helplessly across bare flagstones in black dark, her greaves and empty scabbard clanging upon stone. When she came to a halt, bruised and scratched and breathless, it was a moment before she could collect her senses enough to scramble up, too stunned even for curses.

"Stay where you are Jirel of Joiry," Alaric's voice said calmly out of the blackness. "You cannot escape this hall—we guard every exit with drawn swords. Stand still—and wait."

Jirel got her breath and launched into a blasphemous survey of his ancestry and possible progeny with such vehemence that the dark for several minutes throbbed with her fury. Then she recalled Alaric's suggestion that violence in herself might attract a kindred violence in that strange force called Andred, and she ceased so abruptly that the silence was like a blow upon the ears.

It was a silence full of tense waiting. She could almost feel the patience and the anticipation that beat out upon her from the circle of invisible jailers, and at the thought of what they wanted her blood ran chilly. She looked up blindly into the darkness overhead, certain for a long and dreadful moment that the familiar blast of storm-wind was gathering there to churn the night into chaos out of which Andred's arm would reach. . . .

After a while she said in a voice that sounded unexpectedly small in the darkness:

"Y-you might throw me a pillow. I'm tired of standing and this floor's cold."

To her surprise footsteps moved softly and quite surely across stone, and after a moment a pillow hurtled out of the darkness to thump softly at her feet. Jirel sank upon it thankfully, only to stiffen an instant later and glare about her in the dark, the hair prickling on her neck. So—they could see in the darkness! There had been too much certainty in those footsteps and the accurate toss of the pillow to doubt it. She huddled her shoulders together a little and tried not to think.

The darkness was enormous above her. Age upon age went by, with no sound except her own soft breathing to break that quiet pulsing with waiting and anticipation. Her terror grew. Suppose that dreadful storm-wind should come whooping through the hall again; suppose the bodiless arm should seize her and the mouth come ravening down upon her lips once more. . . . Coldness crept down her spine.

Yes, and suppose it did come again. What use, for her? These slinking abnormalities who were her jailers would never share the treasure with her which they were so avid to find—so avid that they dared evoke this terror by night and brave a death which legend whispered fearfully of, simply that they might possess it.

It—did they know, then, what lay in Andred's terribly guarded box? What conceivable thing could be so precious that men would dare *this* to have it?

And what hope at all for her? If the monstrous thing called Andred did not come tonight—then he would come again some other night, sooner or later, and all nights would find her isolated here as bait for the monster that haunted Hellsgarde. She had boasted without hope when she said her men would follow. They were brave men and they loved her—but they loved living more. No, here was not a man in Joiry who would dare follow where she had failed. She remembered Guy of Garlot's face, and let violence come flooding up in her for a moment. That handsome coward, goading her into this that he might possess the nameless thing he coveted. . . . Well, she would ruin his comely face for him with the crosshilt of her sword—if she lived! She was forgetting. . . .

Slowly the stars wheeled by the arrow-slit windows high up in the darkness of the walls. Jirel sat hugging her knees and watching them. The darkness sighed above her with vagrant drafts, any one of which might be Andred roaring down out of the night. . . .

Well, her captors had made one mistake. How much it might avail her she did not know, but they thought they had disarmed her, and Jirel hugged her greave-sheathed legs in the darkness and smiled a wicked smile, knowing they had not.

It must have been after midnight, and Jirel dozing uneasily with her head on her knees, when a long sigh from the darkness made her start awake. Alaric's voice, heavy with weariness and disappointment, spoke in his nameless language. It occurred to Jirel to wonder briefly that though this seemed to be their mother tongue (for they spoke it under stress and among themselves), yet their speech with her had no taint of accent. It was strange—but she was beyond wondering long about the monstrous folk among whom she had fallen.

Footsteps approached her, walking unerringly. Jirel shook herself awake and stood up, stretching cramped limbs. Hands seized her arms from both sides—at the first grasp, with no groping, though even her dark-accustomed eyes could see nothing. No one bothered to translate Alaric's speech to her, but she realized that they had given up their vigil for the night. She was too drugged with sleep to care. Even her terror had dulled as the endless night hours dragged by. She stumbled along between her captors, making no effort to resist. This was not the time to betray her hidden weapon, not to these people who walked the dark like cats. She could wait until the odds were evener.

No one troubled to strike a light. They went swiftly and unhesitatingly through the blackness, and when stairs rose unexpectedly underfoot Jirel was the only one who stumbled. Up steps, along a cold and echoing hall—and then a sudden thrust that sent her staggering. A stone wall caught her and a door slammed at her back. She whirled, a hot Norman oath smoking on her lips, and knew that she was alone.

Groping, she made out the narrow confines of her prison. There was a cot, a jug of water, a rough door through whose chinks light began to glimmer even as she ran questing hands across its surface. Voices spoke briefly outside, and in a moment she understood. Alaric had summoned one of his apish men to watch her while he and his people slept. She knew it must be a man-at-arms and not one of Alaric's company, for the fellow had brought a lantern with him. She wondered if the guardsmen knew how unerringly their masters walked the darkness—or if they cared. But it no longer seemed strange to her that Alaric dared employ such brutish men. She knew well enough now with what ease he could control them—he and his night-sight and his terrible fearlessness.

Silence fell outside. Jirel smiled a thin smile and leaned into the nearest corner, drawing up one knee. The long, thin-bladed knife she carried between greave and leg slid noiselessly from its sheath. She waited with feline patience, her eyes upon the lighted chinks between the door's planks.

It seemed a long while before the guard ceased his muffled pacing, yawned loudly, tested the bar that fastened the door from without. Jirel's thin smile widened. The man grunted and—she had prayed he would—settled down at last on the floor with his back against the panels of her door. She knew he meant to sleep awhile in the certainty that the door could not be opened without waking him. She had caught her own guards at that trick too often not to expect it now.

Still she waited. Presently the even breath of slumber reached her ears, and she licked her lips and murmured, "Gentle Jesu, let him not wear mail" and leaned to the door. Her knife was thin enough to slide easily between the panels . . . He was not wearing mail—and the blade was razor-keen. He must scarcely have felt it, or known when he died. She felt the knife grate against bone and gave it an expert twist to clear the rib it had grazed, and heard the man give a sudden, startled grunt in his sleep, and then a long sigh . . . He must never have awakened. In a moment blood began to gush through the panels of the door in heavy spurts, and Jirel smiled and withdrew her knife.

It was simple enough to lift the bar with that narrow blade. The difficulty was in opening the door against the dead weight of the man outside, but she accomplished that too, without too much noise—and then the lantern sat waiting for her and the hall was long and empty in the half-dark. She could see the arch of the stairway and knew the way she had come. And she did not hesitate on the way down. She had thought it all out carefully in the darkness of the hall downstairs while she crouched on the cushion and waited for Andred's ravenous storm-blast to come shrieking down above her bent shoulders.

There was no way out. She knew that. Other castles had posterns and windows from which a fugitive might escape, but quicksands surrounded Hellsgarde and the only path to freedom lay along the causeway where Alaric's guard would be watching tonight. And only in minstrels' romances does a lone adventurer escape through a guarded courtyard and a guarded gate.

And too—she had come here for a purpose. It was her duty to find that small treasured box which alone would buy the twenty lives depending on her. She would do that, or die. And perhaps, after all, it was fortunate that the castle had not been empty when she came. Without Alaric, it might never have occurred to her to dare the power of Andred's ghost in order to reach her goal. She realized now that it might well be the only way she would ever succeed. Too many

searchers in the past had ransacked Hellsgarde Castle to
leave her much hope unless great luck attended her. But
Alaric had said it: there was a way—a terrible and
deadly perilous way, but the only hope.

And after all, what chance did she have? To sit
supinely waiting, a helpless decoy, until the night when
Andred's power swooped down to claim her again—or
to seek him out deliberately and challenge him to the
duel. The end would be the same—she must suffer his
presence again, either way. But tonight there was a bare
chance for her to escape with the treasure-casket, or at
least to find it alone and if she lived to hide it and
bargain with Alaric for freedom.

It was a forlorn and futile hope, she knew well. But it
was not in her to sit waiting for death, and this way there
was at least a bare hope for success. She gripped her
bloody knife in one hand and her lantern in the other and
went on down the stairs, cat-footed and quick.

Her little circle of light moving with her across the
cold flags was so tenuous a defense against the dark.
One gust of Andred's storm-wind would puff it out and
the darkness would smash in upon her like a blow. And
there were other ghosts here than Andred's—small,
cold things in the dark just beyond her lantern light. She
could feel their presence as she picked her way across
the great hall, past the quenched logs of the fireplace,
past the crumbling ruins of armor and tapestry, toward
the one spot where she thought she might be surest of
summoning up the dreadful thing she sought.

It was not easy to find. She ranged back and forth for
many minutes with her little circle of light before a
corner of that great black splotch she hunted moved into
the light; beast-shaped, dark as murder itself upon the

flagstones Andred's life-blood spilled two hundred years ago.

Here once before that ravening ghost had taken her; here if anywhere, surely he would come again. She had her underlip firmly between her teeth as she stepped upon that stain, and she was holding her breath without realizing it. She must have stood there for a full minute, feeling the goose-flesh shudder along her limbs, before she could nerve herself for the thing she must do next. But she had come too far to fail herself now. She drew a deep breath and blew out the lifted lantern.

Darkness crashed upon her with the impact of a physical blow, almost squeezing the breath from her body. And now suddenly fright was past and the familiar winy exultation of tension before battle rushed along her limbs and she looked up into the darkness defiantly and shouted to the great vaults of the ceiling, "Come out of Hell, dead Andred! Come if you dare, Andred the Damned!"

Wind—wind and storm and violence! It snatched the words from her lips and the breath from her throat in one tremendous whirling gust that came rushing out of nowhere. And in the instant of its coming, while the wild challenge still echoed on her lips, a ravenous mouth came storming down to silence hers and a great arm smacked down around her shoulders in a blow that sent her reeling as iron fingers dug agonizingly into her arm—a blow that sent her reeling but would not let her fall, for that terrible drag again was sweeping her across the floor with a speed that ran faster than time itself.

She had ducked her head instinctively when she felt the arm seize her, but not soon enough. The heavy mouth had hers, and again the square, wide-set teeth were bruising her lips and the violence of the monstrous kiss made fury bubble up in her sealed throat as she fought in vain against it.

This time the thing was not such a stunning surprise, and she could sense more clearly what was happening to her. As before, the whole violent fury of the attack burst upon her at once—the mouth seized hers and the arm swept her almost off her feet in the same instant. In that instant the unslackening grip around her shoulders rushed her across the dark floor, blinded in the blackness, deafened by the raving wind, muted and dazed by the terrible vehemence of the mouth and the pain of her iron-clawed arm. But she could sense dimly again that walls were closing around her, closer and closer, like a tomb's walls. And as before she was aware of a tremendous force beating about her, a greater violence than any one manifestation of it upon her body; for the mouth, the gripping hand, the arm, the sweeping drag itself were all but parts of that vortex.

And it was indeed a vortex—it was somehow spinning and narrowing as if the whole force that was Andred were concentrating into one tornado-whirl of savage power. Perhaps it was that feeling of narrowing and vortexing rotation which made walls seem to draw close about her. It was all too dimly sensed a thing to put clearly into words, and yet it was terribly real. Jirel, breathless and bruised and stunned with pain and violence, still knew clearly that here in the midst of the great open hall walls were drawing prison-tight about her.

Savagely she slashed at the arm around her shoulders, at the steel-fingered hand digging her arm to the bone. But the angle was an awkward one and she was too dazed to know if she cut flesh or simply stabbed at disembodied force. And the grip did not slacken; the storming mouth still held hers in a kiss so wild and infuriating that she could have sobbed with pure rage.

Those walls were very near . . . her stumbling knees touched stone. She groped dizzily with her free hand and felt walls dripping-damp, close around her. The forward motion had ceased, and the power which was Andred whirled in one concentrated cone of violence that stopped her breath and sent the darkness reeling around her.

Through the haze of her confusion she knew that this, then, must be his own place to which he had dragged her, a place of stone and damp and darkness somewhere *outside*—for they had reached it too quickly for it to be a real place—and yet it was tangible . . . Stone walls cold against her hands, and what were these round and slipping things underfoot?—things that rattled a little as she stumbled among them—bones? Dear God, the bones of other seekers after treasure, who had found what they sought? For she thought the treasure-box must be here, surely, if it were anywhere at all—here in this darkness unreachable save through the very heart of the whirlwind. . . .

Her senses were failing and the whirl that was like the whirl in a tornado's heart seemed to create a vacuum which drew her out of her body in one thin, protesting wisp of self that had no strength to fight. . . .

Somewhere a long way off was her body, hanging limp in the clutch of the iron arm, gasping for breath under a kiss that made reality faint about her, still struggling feebly in some tomb-smelling, narrow place where stone walls dripped and bones turned underfoot—the bones of those who had come before her. . . .

But she was not there. She was a wispy wraith rooted only tenuously in that fainting body, a wraith that reeled out and out in a thin skein to spin on the whirls of tornado-violence pulling her farther and farther and farther away. . . . The darkness was slipping sidewise—the stone walls were a prison no longer, for she was moving up along the great expanding whirl that sucked her out of her body, up and out around widening circles into night-time distances where space and time were not. . . .

Somewhere infinitely far away a foot that was not hers stumbled over something small and square, and a body that was not hers slid to its knees among wet, rattling bones, and a bosom that was not hers bruised itself on the corner of that square something as the tenantless body fell forward among bones upon a wet stone floor. But upon the widening whorls of the vortex the wisp that was Jirel rebelled in its spinning. She must go back—she must remember—there was something—something. . . .

For one fleeting instant she was in her body again, crumpled down upon the stones, arms sprawled about a small square thing that was slimy to the touch. A box—a wet leather box thick with fungus, bound with iron. Andred's box, that for two hundred years searchers had hunted in vain. The box that Andred had died for and that she would die for too—was dying for now in the darkness and the damp among the bones, with violence ravening down to seize her again. . . .

Dimly, as her senses left her for the second time, she heard a dog bark, high and hysterically, from far above.

And another dog answered, and then she heard a man's voice shouting in a tongue she did not know, a wild, exultant shout, choking with triumph. But after that the dizziness of the whirlwind which snatched her out of her body made everything blur, until—until—

Queerly, it was music that brought her back. A lute's strings singing as if madness itself swept wild chords across them. The dwarfed jester's lute, shrieking with music that wakened her out of nowhere into her own fallen body in the dampness and the dark where that hard box-corner bruised her bosom.

And the whirlwind was—uncoiling—from about her. The walls widened until she was no longer aware of their prison closeness and the smell of damp and decay faded from her nostrils. In a dizzy flash of realization she clasped the wet casket to her breast just as the walls faded altogether and she sat up unsteadily, blinking into the dark.

The whirlwind still raved around her, but somehow, strangely, it did not touch her now. No, there was something outside it—some strong force against which it battled—a force that—that—

She was in the dark hall again. Somehow she knew it. And the wild lute-music shrilled and sang, and in some queer way—she saw. It was dark still—but she saw. For a luminous glow was generating itself in a ring around her and by its ghostlight she was aware—scarcely through sight—of familiar faces spinning past her in a wide, whirling ring. A witch dance, round and round. . . . Alaric's lined face flashed by, blazing with exultation; Damara's white-ringed eyes glared blindly into the dark. She saw the two boys whirl past, the light of hell itself luminous on their faces. There was a wild bark, and one of the greyhounds loped by her and away, firelight from no earthly flame glaring in its eyes, its tongue lolling in a canine grin of ecstasy. Round and round her through that luminous glow which was scarcely light the mad circle spun. And ever the lute-strings wailed and sang with a wilder music than strings can ever have sung before, and the terrible joy on every face—yes, even upon the dogs'—was more frightening than even Andred's menace had been.

Andred—Andred. . . . The power of his volcano-force spun above her now, with a strength that stirred the red hair against her cheeks and a raving of wind through which the lute music screamed high. But it was not the dull force that had overwhelmed her. For this maniac dance that spun round and round through the dark was building up a climax of cumulative strength that she could feel as she knelt there, hugging the slimy box. She thought the very air sang with tension and stress. That circle was reeling counterwise to the spin of Andred's vortexing force, and Andred was weakening. She could feel him slackening above her in the dark. The music shrieked louder above the failing storm-wind and the fearful joy upon those faces whirling past told her why. Somehow they were overpowering him. Something in the dwarf's mad lute-strings, something in the spinning of their dance was breaking down the strength of Andred's centuries-old violence. She could feel it weakening as she crouched there with the casket hugged bruisingly to her bosom.

And yet—was it this precious casket that they fought for? No one had a glance to spare for the crouching girl or the burden she hugged. Every face was lifted raptly,

every eye stared blindly and exultantly into the upper
dark as if the thing that was Andred was visible and—
and infinitely desirable. It was a lust for that thing upon
their faces that made joy so vivid there. Jirel's brain had
almost ceased recording sensation in the bewilderment
of what she watched.

When the dance ended she scarcely knew it. Lulled
into a dizzy trance by the mad spinning of the dancers,
she was almost nodding on her. knees in their center,
feeling her brain whirl with their whirling—feeling the
motion slow about her so imperceptibly that nothing but
the whirl itself registered on her mind. But the dancers
were slackening—and with them, the whirl above. The
wind no longer raved through the dark; it was a slow
sigh now, growing softer and gentler as the circle of
dancers ceased to spin. . . .

And then there was a great, soft, puffing sigh from
the darkness above her that blew out her awareness like
a candleflame. . . .

Daylight fingering through the arrow-slits touched
Jirel's closed lids. She awoke painfully, blinking in the
light. Every muscle and bone of her supple body ached
from the buffeting of last night's storm and violence,
and the cold stones were hard beneath her. She sat up,
groping by instinct for her knife. It lay a little distance
off, rusting with last night's blood. And the casket—the
casket! . . .

Panic swelling in her throat quieted in an instant as
she saw that precious, molding thing lying on its side at
her elbow. A little thing, its iron hinges rusty, its leather
whitened and eaten with rot from two centuries in a
nameless, dripping place; but safe, unopened. She

picked it up, shaking it experimentally. And she heard the softest shifting within, a sound and weight like finest flour moving gently.

A rustle and a sigh from beyond brought her head up, and she stared around her in the shadows of the halls. In a broad, uneven circle the bodies of last night's dancers lay sprawled. Dead? No, slow breathing stirred them as they lay, and upon the face of the nearest—it was Damara—was a look of such glutted satiety that Jirel glanced away in disgust. But they all shared it. She had seen revelers asleep after a night of drunken feasting with not half such surfeit, such almost obscene satisfaction upon their faces as Alaric's drugged company wore now. Remembering that obscure lusting she had seen in their eyes last night, she wondered what nameless satiety they had achieved in the dark after her own consciousness went out. . . .

A footfall sounded upon stone behind her and she spun halfway round, rising on one knee and shifting the knife-hilt firmer in her fist. It was Alaric, a little unsteady on his feet, looking down upon her with a sort of half-seeing abstraction. His scarlet tunic was dusty and rumpled as if he had slept in it all night upon the floor and had only just risen. He ran a hand through his ruffled hair and yawned, and looked down at her with a visible effort at focusing his attention.

"I'll have your horse brought up," he said, his eyes sliding indifferently away from her even as he spoke. "You may go now."

Jirel gaped up at him, her lips parting in amazement over white teeth. He was not watching her. His eyes had shifted focus and he was staring blindly into some delightful memory that had blotted out Jirel's very existence. And upon his face that look of almost obscene satiety relaxed every feature until even his sword-gash mouth hung loose.

"B-but—" Jirel blinked and clutched at the mildewed box she had risked her life for. He came back into focus for an impatient instant to say carelessly:

"Oh—that! Take the thing."

"You—you know what it is? I thought you wanted—"

He shrugged. "I could not have explained to you last night what it was I wanted of—Andred. So I said it was the treasure we sought—you could understand that. But as for that rotting little box—I don't know or care what lies inside. I've had—a better thing . . ." And his remembering eyes shifted again to escape hers and stare blissfully into the past.

"Then why did you—save me?"

"Save you?" He laughed. "We had no thought of you or your treasure in what we—did—last night. You have served your purpose—you may go free."

"Served—what purpose?"

Impatiently for an instant he brought himself wholly back out of his remembering dream to say:

"You did what we were holding you for—called up Andred into our power. Lucky for you that the dogs sensed what happened after you had slipped off to dare the ghost alone. And lucky for us, too. I think Andred might not have come even to take you, had he sensed our presence. Make no doubt of it—he feared us, and with good reason."

Jirel looked up at him for a long instant, a little chill creeping down her spine, before she said in a shaken whisper:

"What—are you?" And for a moment she almost hoped he would not answer. But he smiled, and the look of deformity deepened upon his face.

"A hunter of undeath," he said softly. "A drinker of undeath, when I can find it. . . . My people and I lust after that dark force which the ghosts of the violent dead engender, and we travel far sometimes between—feastings." His eyes escaped hers for an instant to stare gloatingly into the past. Still looking with that unfocused gaze, in a voice she had not heard before from him, he murmured, "I wonder if any man who has not tasted it could guess the utter ecstasy of drinking up the undeath of a strong ghost . . . a ghost as strong as Andred's . . . feeling that black power pouring into you in deep drafts as you suck it down—a thirst that strengthens as you drink—feel—darkness—spreading through every vein more sweetly than wine, more intoxicating. . . . To be drunk on undeath—a joy almost unbearable."

Watching him, Jirel was aware of a strong shudder that rose in the pit of her stomach and ran strongly and shakingly along her limbs. With an effort she tore her gaze away. The obscene ecstasy that Alaric's inward-looking eyes dwelt upon was a thing she would not see even in retrospect, through another's words and eyes. She scrambled to her feet, cradling the leather box in her arm, averting her eyes from his.

"Let me go, then," she said in a lowered voice, obscurely embarrassed as if she had looked inadvertently upon something indescribable. Alaric glanced up at her and smiled.

"You are free to go," he said, "but waste no time returning with your men for vengeance against the force we imposed on you.'' His smile deepened at her little twitch of acknowledgment, for that thought had been in her mind. ''Nothing holds us now at Hellsgarde. We will leave today on—another search. One thing before you go—we owe you a debt for luring Andred into our power, for I think he would not have come without you. Take a warning away with you, lady.''

''What is it?'' Jirel's gaze flicked the man's briefly and fell again. She would not look into his eyes if she could help it. ''What warning?''

''Do not open that box you carry.''

And before she could get her breath to speak he had smiled at her and turned away, whistling for his men. Around her on the floor Jirel heard a rustling and a sigh as the sleepers began to stir. She stood quiet for an instant longer, staring down in bewilderment at the small box under her arm, before she turned to follow Alaric into the outer air.

Last night was a memory and a nightmare to forget. Not even the dead men still on their ghastly guard before the door could mar her triumph now.

Jirel rode back across the causeway in the strong light of morning, moving like a rider in a mirage between blue skies and blue reflecting waters. Behind her Hellsgarde Castle was a vision swimming among the mirroring pools of the marsh. And as she rode, she remembered.

The vortex of violence out of which she had snatched this box last night—the power and terror of the thing that had treasured it so long . . . what lay within? Something akin to—Andred? Alaric might not know, but he had guessed . . . His warning still sounded in her ears.

She rode awhile with bent brows, but presently a wicked little smile began to thin the red lips of Joiry's sovereign lady. Well . . . she had suffered much for Guy of Garlot, but she thought now that she would not smash in his handsome, grinning face with her sword-hilt as she had dreamed so luxuriously of doing. No . . . she would have a better vengeance. . . .

She would hand him a little iron-bound leather box.